Olive E Dana

Under friendly eaves

Olive E. Dana

Under friendly eaves

ISBN/EAN: 9783337056896

Printed in Europe, USA, Canada, Australia, Japan

Cover: Foto ©Andreas Hilbeck / pixelio.de

More available books at **www.hansebooks.com**

UNDER FRIENDLY EAVES

BY

OLIVE E. DANA

"It seems as if the heroes have done almost all for the
world that they can do, and not much more can come till
common men awake and take their common tasks."
—*Phillips Brooks.*

"The healing of the world
Is in its nameless saints. Each separate star
Seems nothing, but a myriad scattered stars
Break up the night and make it beautiful."
—*Bayard Taylor.*

AUGUSTA, MAINE
BURLEIGH & FLYNT, PRINTERS
1894

CONTENTS.

PROEM.

Just as they came to me, I write them here,—
   These homely tales of simple, friendly folk
Whose hidden hearth-fires breathe the wreathèd smoke
   That tells of home, warmth, love, when skies are drear:
Whose tranquil faith and unstrained virtue calm
   Life's fevered pulse like some familiar psalm:
Who make us feel how royal goodness is,
   How worthless all men gather, lacking this;
Who keep for us, despite Time's swift mischance,
   Our dear New England's best inheritance.

O. E. D.

AUGUSTA, October 16, 1894.

UNDER FRIENDLY EAVES.

MISS ESTHER.

Close beside a range of low, lovely mountains that seem to impart to the place something of their own permanence and serenity, even when the whirr of the mill-wheels is loudest, the crowd of employes at the factory gates and along dingy Broad Street thickest and noisiest, Ashland lifts its spires and chimneys, breathing the hot air of its activities into the cool, calm air of the hills.

It is a quaint little city, with Swift River dashing through its midst, heaping masses of foam upon its rocky shores, and turning the wheels of a score of manufactories, lesser and greater. Shoddy tenements, showy stores, and shops of all grades have sprung up inevitably around them, now and then a finer block or statelier residence, or the square tower of a schoolhouse, giving promise of better things.

2

The older portion of the town is on the other side of the river, and farther away, opposite the hills, upon which it gains thereby the larger outlook. Its streets, too, are higher and wider, and the old-fashioned houses stand far apart along elm-shaded roads that in a more aspiring place would be called "avenues," and are even now taking that name in the speech of the younger generation.

In this part, however, is the railroad station, for Ashland is the terminus of a well known road, and this arrangement, while it brings a daily stir and renewal of life to Old Ashland, as the older part of the town is called, gives the visitor or traveller a far pleasanter impression of the little city than he would at first receive if it were otherwise. For on his right, just far enough removed to render their less pleasing features less conspicuous, are the blocks and stores, the storied mills, the clustered houses, and the background of blue hills, and on the left, and nearer, the wide home-like streets and comfortable mansions that New Englanders made sure of a century ago.

It was in this guise that Ashland showed itself to the passengers of the late afternoon train one day in early winter, its rows of glowing windows on the one hand, and the scattered home-lights so near by on the other, making cheerful welcome, signals as the long train rumbled slowly into the open station.

To one pair of eyes, looking out steadily yet absently upon town, and hills, and glowing sunset skies, the scene was familiar enough. Sixty years had been spent in this environment, which seemed still to compass the most and best of life's duties, opportunities, joys. Just why, even Miss Esther Mortimer herself could hardly have told you.

She watched, to-night, with eyes that had an unanswered question in them, the lights flash out, one after another, and the streets open below, till, as the train jerked itself to a standstill, the whole village showed itself with unexpected distinctness.

There is a connection, slenderer and subtler than causation, between the outer and the inner vision, as if the gates of sight swinging wider, set open some psychical avenue, and let in an unlooked for perception or aspiration. Some such message might have come to Miss Esther, for a new satisfaction and a new eagerness came together into her gray eyes, and she sat quite still though her fellow travellers were jostling each other in the car aisles. Was it that bit of purple sky changing to softest gray above the darkening hills, the amber of the clouds, dispersing now and fading slowly, that detained her? Or the fine lines of that piece of hemlock woods,—her own—left standing at the right of the largest factory, with the slenderer birches beside them, and the sunset light shining through? Or it may have been just the effective grouping of the village lights, near and far, and the fine effect of the factory windows,—there were two or three of the larger buildings unlighted, but these were not noticeable, at dusk,—and it was, indeed, upon this portion of the town that her eyes lingered longest.

But Miss Mortimer's gray horses, that had been stamping on the other side of the platform since the train had just whistled, betrayed a livelier impatience, and James Stackpole, himself, their staid driver, was as restive as they, Miss Mortimer could see.

"And Martha Storlett will think I have given out on the journey, or else stayed over. I don't know but James thinks I'm not able to get out, for he's coming to look for me. I must go, though I've found just what I was looking for,—all mapped out and planned. Well, it will keep, now I've got it."

With which enigmatical words Miss Esther left the car, and, a moment later, alert, self-possessed and kindly, was entering her carriage, and giving her checks to the vigilant James, while ten minutes afterwards she stood in her own hall, shaking hands with Martha Storlett and hoping her supper had not been kept waiting.

"The train *was* rather late, and I—didn't hurry."

"And how are you, Miss Esther? Any better? asked Martha, a note of anxiety in her brisk voice.

"No worse, certainly," said Miss Mortimer, with a smile singularly sweet for a face so reserved. "I'll tell you all about it after supper, Martha. Just now I do believe I'm hungry."

And Martha, reassured more by her mistress's voice and manner than by her words or her pale and really weary face, returned to her own realm, content.

An hour later the two women sat together in a room whose quaint, well-kept furniture,— softened into ease by luxurious accessories of a later date, and by a cheerfully tranquil atmosphere intensified by the open fire, the rows of books, the orderly litter of periodicals, the pungent fragrance of crimson pinks,—seemed in keeping with each, and harmonized their unlikenesses, as long-wonted things and the atmosphere they make, will often do.

"You want to know all about it, Martha, I suppose?" queried Miss Mortimer from her easy-chair.

And Martha, plying her knitting-needles vigorously in a straight-backed rocker, nodded assent, adding, in a disapproving interrogation :

"You went to the hotel?"

"No, not to stay. I had lunch there,—the train gets in at noon, you know, and I left my things there at first. But,—Martha, do you remember Mary Duncan?"

"Mary Henderson that was? Yes, indeed."

"Well," went on Miss Mortimer, clasping her hands and gazing into the grate,—"You see, I had to have a veil,—my last one gave out last week and Miss Slocum never has anything of that sort one would wear,—so I went into Record's to get it and to leave an order. That was on my way to Dr. Prescott. I saw Madame first, and she called a young girl to pin the veil,—it was unmanageable, they always are. I did not notice her at first, save that she had a soft voice that somehow seemed familiar, and a nice manner. But when I turned to look at her I stood shock-still. 'Mary Henderson!' I said, and put out both hands.

I hadn't had my lunch then, nor seen the doctor, and I think I was a little weak and confused.

" 'Mary Henderson Duncan,' she said. 'That was my mother's name.' She looked pleased, but she wouldn't take the least advantage of my Rip Van Winkle blunder. 'Mary Henderson,' I said, 'was my dear friend,—my *dearest* friend. And I haven't seen or heard from her in years. Does she live in town, and will you give me her address? I should like to call on her.' So she told me where they lived, and said,—she is as proud as she is pretty,—'She will be very glad to see Miss Mortimer.' And I came away and went to the doctor's—I'll tell you about that next,—and the first person I saw in his reception room was Mary herself. She had her youngest child there, his eyes are bad. And she knew me, and found out that I was at the St. James, and guessed what my errand was, and made me telephone for my things and go home with her. I had the best visit, Martha,—with just her and the children, —their father died, you know, years ago. Yes, they are poor, that is they maintain themselves, with her little income. And Mary herself helps; she is secretary and half-manager, I should think, of one of the charitable societies.

It just suits her, and brings her in the way of helping a great many people,—all sorts, in all sorts of ways. And I don't suppose they can afford to despise the small salary she gets, either, though she doesn't work for that."

"But about the doctor, what did he say?" said Martha, smoothing her black silk apron and waiting for what was to her, relatively of much more importance.

"Oh! he said it wasn't a settled disease, he thought, though it might easily become so, at my age, and with my heredity and habits. And he said I must avoid exposure, of course, —I always do,—and fatigue. And that I must have diversion and companionship, interesting occupation, cheerful society and all that. Oh, and that I must take nourishment frequently. He proposed Florida, or California, this winter, and Europe next summer. Wanted to know if I hadn't relatives or friends in the South. Suggested a sanitarium, in Colorado, I believe, but admitted afterwards that a change was in no wise necessary, if the other conditions were met."

"And what will you do?" asked Martha, eagerly. "There's your cousin John in San Francisco, and Harry in Carolina. They'd be delighted if you'd visit them."

"But I am not going to,—now!" said Miss Mortimer, with vigorous emphasis. "Home is best, sick or well, for me, especially when I'm half-sick. Why, Martha Storlett, do you know what tiresome, inane, nerve-wearing work it is to visit, visit, visit, a season through? And do you know that any number of maids, and preparatory telegrams, and fees, and 'tips,' and what not, wouldn't make me so comfortable as I am this blessed minute?"

"I know it," said Martha, in doubtful agreement,—"but the society, and the amusement, and all the rest of it,—you can't get those in Ashland?"

"Depends on what you mean by 'em," said Miss Mortimer, laconically.

"Martha," she said presently, after a pause, —a perplexed silence to Martha, a thoughtful one to her,—"Martha, do you know a pretty, dark-eyed girl, slender and rather sober, that goes to our own church? She wears, I remember, a blue suit, dark blue and very plain, and sits in a side-pew."

Then as Martha shook her head, she went on,——

"She was on the train to-day. I think she gives music lessons somewhere not far away. I was thinking that if I knew her well enongh,

I'd ask her to pour chocolate at some of my teas this winter. She'd be just the one, I fancy. But Frances Butler will do."

"*Your teas!*" ejaculated Martha. "I thought you had got to keep quiet and take care of yourself, and—have a good time, if you could this winter."

"That's just what I'm going to do," said Miss Esther, calmly," and the 'afternoons' are a part of it."

"Martha," she went on, after a moment, in a changed tone, "do you know they say it's going to be a very hard winter, even here in Ashland? That three of the largest mills have stopped running, that trade is very dull, and that help is being constantly turned away from the stores and offices? Martha, I cannot bear to estimate how many people there must be in Ashland, our old Ashland, who literally will not be able to afford three meals a day, or two, this winter! And Martha, how much idle capital, yes, *capital*, that is accumulating at a comfortable rate, do you suppose is represented on this street? No, I shall not tell you; you wouldn't believe it. I am ashamed of it, myself. And you might multiply it by three, and not count all Ashland's unused property."

"But, dear Miss Esther," Martha interjected, anxiously, as Miss Mortimer paused for breath. "You cannot help it! You are willing to do your part. It may not be so bad as you think. And you are not to blame. What can you do?"

"I can do my part," Miss Mortimer answered. "I am not sure yet what that is—all of it. But I will have my teas,—I think, somehow, they will help us to find out."

"Indeed, Martha," she said, eagerly, as the other was about to protest, "I must have my way. I do not think Dr. Prescott would like to have me crossed. And didn't he say I must have interesting occupation and society?"

"I do not see," she exclaimed, in a moment, "how people, rich people, can bear to economize this year of all years! I know we are talked to as if it were a cardinal virtue. But if we economize in expenditures that are everyday matters, for us, somebody, a good many somebodies, must starve! Why, Martha, I fancy what I should spend this winter, if it were no more than usual, and just for my ordinary luxuries,—*I* didn't put the two words together, first,—would make a difference, so far as it goes. And if I choose to make it a little more than usual, in certain quarters,—I shall take care whom it goes to, you may be sure,—and do my best not to have it a dull winter in Ashland, socially speaking, why it may even make the other dullness a little less terrible, don't you think? At any rate, I sha'n't draw on my banker for twice what I usually use in a season and go off to California or Carolina with it!"

So it came about that the winter in Ashland society did not promise to be so very dull after all. It was the old story of the ball once set rolling—there were a score of hands eager to keep it in motion, whose owners, most of them, did not guess on what a beneficent mission it had been started, or how near the game came to being "in earnest."

People did notice that Miss Mortimer was going into company more than usual,—she was giving a series of delightful "At Homes." One couldn't afford to miss them, and every-one, really, was there. They were so charm-ing! Something new or unusual every week; you never could tell what she would have next. Some of the things *were* odd, and some-times very "common" people took part, but Miss Mortimer could afford to do those things.

Some of this comment, indeed, most of it, at one time or another, came to Miss Mortimer's own ears, but she only smiled and went on her way serenely, and went all the more confidently to invite May Burton, the janitor's pretty, gifted daughter, to sing the next week, stopping meanwhile to ask the earnest little artist, Jenny Fay, to spend a few days at "The Oaks" a little later.

"I must see your work," she said, graciously. "I used to draw myself. And my friends will enjoy it."

Of course there were those among Miss Mortimer's guests who recognized these young people as her protégées, and divined her kindly purposes, and made both them and herself conscious of their knowledge of these facts. But Miss Mortimer's tact and her spirited repartee never failed to be equal to the occasion, and, for the most part, her intent was too brave and genuine, and the spirit of good-will and brotherhood it evoked too potent to allow of other than the friendliest comment.

"They think I don't know they say I have all sorts," she said one day to Martha. "That's just what I mean to have. Ashland people had pretty nearly forgotten they were of one flesh, or that there could be anything in common between some folks and other folks."

"And they find, now and then, there aint such a great difference between 'em, after all," added Martha, smiling grimly. "But where's that girl you were speaking of? Did you ever find out her name, Miss Mortimer? Or anything more about her."

"Her name," said Miss Esther, briefly, is Henderson, Ruth Henderson."

And Martha asked no more. Her ready and still sensitive perception supplied what had not been told, and she awaited further developments with a half-resentful interest.

The Hendersons were an old Ashland family, of whom Mary Duncan and her family, and their young cousin Ruth were now the only. representatives. John Henderson had been, as everyone believed, Miss Esther's lover; but so tacit had been the relation, and so reticent and, apparently, heart-whole, was she when he left Ashland, and her, and soon afterward married, that no one had questioned, or, openly, pitied her. And even loyal Martha could hardly be sure with what feeling John Henderson's daughter would be regarded, or whether the tenderness Miss Mortimer had always for young, aspiring souls, struggling in adverse conditions, would be less or greater than its wont, now that she knew her young neighbor's lineage.

"We shall see what we shall see," she said to herself, soberly, and gave herself with even

more than usual ardor to the tasks that fell to
her share.   In truth, these tasks were not few
nor slight.   She had never heard Mr. Hale's
fine phrase, "the magic of together," but she
knew,—as she said to herself,—that "when
people got together, and especially when they
were in the habit of it, in the right sort of
way, something was pretty sure to be done,
and commonly, several somethings."   And
indeed so it proved.   There were many pro-
jects on foot, some of them really charities,
many of them only organized, yet unobtrusive, helpfulness.   The full hands on the one
side were offering themselves to the empty
ones on the other.   And not, as I said, in
charity alone, save in its spirit.   One or two
things Miss Mortimer had hardly dared to
hope for, certainly not to suggest, were accomplished ere the Candlemas sun had set.
The directors of the Ascot mills, at their mid-
winter meeting, voted themselves to advance
the capital necessary to resume operations
therein, and to hold themselves responsible
for their continuance.   That was the turning-
point in the battle for Ashland, even had not
several lesser corporations followed suit, as
they did, immediately.

And the societies, and boards, and guilds,
which had organized for the relief of "the

unemployed," must needs turn their energies into other channels, or rather, seek new and wiser methods of helpfulness, which was, on the whole, a far better thing for them all. It is doubtless more prosaic to teach in an evening school, to help sustain a working-girls' club, or a home-culture society, or a class in sewing or wood-carving, than actually to relieve the suffering and destitute, but who can doubt that the former is the more fruitful work, deeper and farther-reaching in its effects?

And it was when effort had reached this stage in its evolution from the germ of "willingness" nurtured by Miss Mortimer, that an acquaintance with Ruth Henderson ·really begun. Ruth was a teacher in one of the guild classes, and an officer of the girls' club, which met at Miss Mortimer's home. Martha watched the growing intimacy doubtfully.

"If she's satisfied, I s'pose I ought to be," she said to herself. "And truly, I do believe that one girl's done her more good, somehow, than all the rest. She was picking up pretty well, though, before. I wonder what that doctor thinks, now? People generally know what they need, themselves, especially when they've an eye out for other folks' needs, too.

But I don't see what that trouble between her and John Henderson was. I don't suppose I ever *shall* know."

And she never did, though she lived to hear John Henderson's name spoken many times, and with warm and affectionate remembrance, by both the younger and the older woman. Nor did she ever know of the little package of time-stained letters, or the worn diary, bearing date of years long ended, that Ruth, after she had come to be half-daughter, half-sister in the house, gave one day into Miss Esther's hands.

"For," Ruth said, "I think they belong to you now."

HIS LAST BATTLE.

The dusky air was sweet with the breath of syringas, just opening their snowy blooms in the front yards, and now and then was blown the heavier fragrance of lilacs, or the finer scent of the honeysuckle, from some fence corner where such rank growths still flourished. But the shrubs themselves, and even the paling behind which they stood, were hidden in the gathering mist which, growing denser as the twilight deepened, obscured even the dwellings set far. apart, as in dignified reserve, on either side the long, wide street.

The village lights shone dimly through the vapors, and even in the flickering glare of the street-lamps, dotting infrequently the long highway, the forms and faces of the passers-by were blurred and indistinct. Pedestrians peered inquisitively into their neighbors' faces, as they met on the pavement, thankful for any obvious peculiarity of form or gait that made recognition easy.

With a step which had something of uncertainty in it, too eager to be listless, too feeble to be quite expectant, yet which had a certain precision and rhythmic regularity, a man, tall and gaunt, came down the sidewalk and made his way through the little knot of loungers that the evening mail had attracted, and up the steps of the postoffice. His face looked pale and careworn when the light fell on it as he entered the building, and the little group about the delivery window parted to let him make his inquiry out of turn. He waited with an anxious unexpectancy, banished in a moment as the postmaster reached him an official looking letter. He grasped it in his right hand—his left sleeve was pinned, empty, across his breast—and turned hurriedly away.

Through the misty street he retraced his steps, clutching the letter closely. By and by he turned into a vacant entrance, before which a light burned brightly, stopped, looked nervously about him, and tore open the envelope, thrusting it under his empty sleeve while he drew forth the letter it contained. He read it hastily, then slowly, then re-read it again as if unable to comprehend its import. Presently, with a face more haggard than before, he returned the sheet to its envelope, thrust it into his pocket, stepped out of the doorway, and went on. Hurriedly at first, until he was out of the village, then, despite the fog that was almost rain, laggingly and aimlessly.

A crowd of confused, bitter, bewildered thoughts was in his brain, which yet seemed almost vacant, too. As well it might. Had not a hope gone out of it? A hope that had sustained mind and heart, and even the feeble body itself, for many a day?

Why had he let himself hope, he questioned. He was aware that there was a flaw in his papers, that his proofs of honorable service and discharge were not technically complete. There was a discrepancy in the dates, probably the error of a copying clerk, possibly a mistake in the entry or its transmission.

"A technical error," the pension agent had called it, which might or might not be a legal one, and most likely was not; corroborating the opinion of Squire Burns, the village lawyer. The authorities, only, could decide it, and it was best, by all means, to submit it to them. All had agreed in this. And he had done so.

But if they had only told him at once, or sooner. He did not build on the hope of a pension so much at first. Not until he had grown older and feebler, and could do and bear less, and his wife had been ill; not till they began to fall behind, and Phemie had had to give up her school to take care of her mother, and one of the horses died and Sam had begun to question whether they had not better give up farming altogether, and leave him free to earn in some other way. He had been away through the late winter and early spring, and had come home only a few weeks before, for another season's effort. And this might have tided them over the shallows.

It meant so much to them. Independence, home, comfort, hope for the future, and maybe, with and by means of these, for the older ones, health, and life itself. Youth could hold its own, at least, though Phemie was hardly fit to face the world; but age has a sore fight, single-handed. And he smiled grimly at the literalness of his metaphor.

So he wandered on, hurt and hopeless, and bewildered, thinking his bitter, dreary thoughts. He did not think of the time, even when the nine o'clock bell rang, though he knew, if he had recollected, that they would be looking for him at home long before that hour. It did occur to him by and by, but he neither turned nor hastened. How could he go home and tell them? They would have to know when he went—if he went. But he could not go home to tell Martha and Phemie and Sam *that*.

The road turned abruptly just there, met by a stream, not wide, but deep and turbulent. Outside of New England it would perhaps be called a river, but here it was only Stony Brook. A bridge spanned it here, in continuance of the highway—a toll-bridge, and Jonas Rand put his hand into his pocket instinctively, but his fingers met that letter, and he withdrew them empty. He must not spend pennies needlessly, now.

He looked back toward the village; but its lights had for him no beckoning radiance. Eastward he turned his eyes, where among the scattered home-lights, one by one disappearing, was one familiar and dear, that had been his lode-star through toilsome years. But he shook his head mechanically. Not there—yet. Was there no place for him then? For earth seemed suddenly cold and uninviting. Hark! Below him Stony Brook, hurrying on in its reckless haste, swollen by the spring rains, shouted, "Come, come, come!" Why should he not obey?

How long he stood there he never knew. Not long, doubtless, measuring the time by hours. But he had been in battles whose smoke had not lifted from sun to sun, and from sunset to dawn, and to dark again, that were not so long, so dark, so fateful. But it was over at last, and he turned, no longer bewildered nor uncertain, but saying in his heart:

"No! As I am a man, and God made me one, aye, and by His own providence this man, baffled and helpless as I am—a man I will be! And in this world of His I will stay till He calls me out of it. The rest He will take care of."

Between Stony Brook and the Rand farm lay a lonely stretch of road, but it was neither long nor lonesome to Jonas Rand that night. A solemn peace, that left no room for forebodings, a thankfulness so warm and deep that it was almost gladness, filled his heart. The mist, unobserved by him, had thinned and lifted. As he turned homeward, a star shone out of the parting clouds, joined, as he went on, by another and another, till the blue sky was studded with them. The west wind stirred softly the roses by his porch, and sent a shower of fragrant drops into his face as he went up the steps.

Though it was late, and, as he had expected, the family had waited for him, it somehow did not seem to be wholly on his account. Nor were they so anxious as he had anticipated, to hear the news he might have brought. He had seen them often far more disturbed and expectant. Something else had excited them—it could not be his mood reflected in their faces —and not unpleasantly.

"You are late, father, and you must be well tired out. Take his coat, Phemie, then run out and see if the tea is like to be hot. He must have something warm right away," said Mrs. Rand, leaving her own rocking-chair to bring his worn dressing-gown and slippers.

"And we've had callers," said Sam. "They wanted to see you, but couldn't wait any longer. At least one of 'em did."

"Ah !" said the father, thinking how warm and bright the fire and lamplight were, how pretty Phemie was growing, how strong Sam looked, and how manly—that home was sweet and life good, and even mother looked better than a day or two ago. What if—well, what if any great sorrow had come to any of them that night! God forbid! And had He not? How good He was !

"Ah? I met some one at the foot of the lane, but it was so dark there in the orchard I couldn't tell who it was," he went on.

Phemie had turned away, and no one spoke for a moment, then Sam said:

"Yes, we've had two visitors. You haven't seen John Freeman lately, have you? Well, he's been over to-night. And—I never thought much about it before—it always seemed such a worthless piece of land to us, for all the wood-lot—but he wants to buy that heater-piece, between our south meadow and his pasture land. You know it's really a sizeable piece of land, and got some pretty good timber on it. And it just evens up his land, and ours, finally, t'other way. So he's willing to pay a good fair price for it, out and out. I don't know exactly how much, but about what it's worth, and enough to give us a good lift. Enough to set us square with the world, and give us something to help ourselves with, besides. That is, if you're willing to let it go. It's as you say, of course."

For the father had raised himself for a moment, as if in dismay, had lifted his hand as if to stay him, and even Sam could but be startled by the pallor of his face. But it passed in a moment, and he answered, throwing all his strength into the words:—

"Willing? Well, I should think so. I've often looked at that heater-piece, and thought

3

what a queer survey it was that divided the land so. But I never supposed John cared enough about it to buy it. It'll be a great help to us, and not hurt the farm any to speak of, either. I'd a' been willing to let a good bit of land go, to square us round this spring. I wish I'd seen John. Probably I met him there in the orchard lane."

"No," answered Sam, relieved, but wishing his father were less thin and white, "he went two hours ago. They go to bed with the chickens, over to Freemans'. I guess that was Loring Burns. He's been here, too."

"Loring? Wanted to see me, didn't he?"

He spoke eagerly and less gladly. Burns & Son were the village lawyers, whom he had consulted. Probably they had heard, too. Their homestead adjoined the Rand place, and both the elder and the younger man sometimes dropped in of an evening in a neighborly way, or to talk over his claim.

But Sam—what was the boy smiling at?— answered slowly:

"Well, no. He didn't speak of having any errand, at least, not to me, when I went to the door. Fact, his business seemed to be with Phemie."

A perception of the young lawyer's "errand" came at last to the father's mind. To this new state of affairs he must adjust himself slowly, and he expressed his surprise only in a slow, involuntary "Oh!" while Sam smiled again, and Phemie retreated to look after "that tea."

But even its medicinal quality could not avert the consequence of the evening's exposure and the shock of his disappointment, resolutely put by though as it had been at last, and now well might be, in the brightening family fortunes. Morning found him weak, stiff and feverish, and with a painful cough, which assumed so suddenly a serious character that physician and family alike, ignorant of his vigil, found it hard to account for it. It was when a week had passed, and he had begun to mend, that Phemie found in his pocket the letter, whose existence had been unknown by them hitherto, and read it forthwith, first to herself, and then to her mother and brother.

"Just as I expected," said Sam.

"I never felt as though 'twould come," said Mrs. Rand.

"And I'm sure I didn't," said Phemie. "I thought he looked all given out that night. We won't say anything about it till he does. And I believe we'd better not say anything about its being Memorial Day, unless he does. It may make him feel badly after this. Dear me, there comes Gracie Barrows, to rehearse her piece to me, now. I'm afraid he'll hear us."

She took the girl into the parlor, and closed the door; but Gracie asked in a moment or two for a drink of water, and the door was left unlatched when they returned to their task, so that the sweet, girlish voice, clear and distinct, floated into the sick man's room. He turned his head to listen. "What's that?"

"One of Phemie's scholars rehearsing a piece to her for the exercises this afternoon."

"Decoration Day, aint it? Have the children carried over any flowers?"

"What we had," replied Mrs. Rand, uneasily.

"Those wild plum blossoms would go in well with the rest, and I know where there's a lot of honeysuckles, over in the meadow, by the east woods, there. You'd better tell Sam to go get some and carry."

And left alone, he listened again to the lines the girl was repeating, words that fell on his ears like balm, and lingering in his hearing, lulled him to sleep:

> "He serves his country best
> Who lives pure life, and doeth righteous deed,
> And walks straight paths, however others stray,
> And leaves his sons, as uttermost bequest,
> A stainless record which all men may read.
> This is the better way."

Stony Brook had lost its spring-tide turbulence, and went singing softly over the pebbles, where from his windows Jason Rand saw it, hastening seaward, again. Sam wondered why, in the hay field, his father should stop and look and listen, when their work took them near its banks.

Phemie, when she had gone, at harvest time, to her new home, wondered that, when her father came in to see her there, and was shown through her pretty rooms, he should look from each window at the same familiar hills and meadows with the same slender stream threading its way between them.

And when, by and by, childish hands led him along the well-worn paths between the homes, the little guide would go slowly, puzzled that grandpa should always stop, midway, to look at the brook at the foot of the old orchards and to listen to its song.

They laid him to rest, one day, in God's Acre, overlooking its shores. A fluttering flag shows that it is a soldier's grave, and Stony Brook—conscious of its secret—sings for him a tender requiem.

A THANKSGIVING DISTRIBUTION.

The November sun, half an hour high, shone through breaking clouds on the long, wind-swept height long known as Meeting-house Hill. It was reflected from the eastern windows of the bare, ancient, white-painted structure, that gave the hill its name, and it gleamed very brightly into the cheerful sitting-room at the old Fields farm, where Miss Lois and Miss Lucretia sat, after their cosy breakfast, reading their morning chapter. "The Fields girls," they were still called, though Miss Lois, the younger of the two, was nearing sixty. The old farmhouse, and the many-acred, if somewhat sterile farm, had, in Nathan Fields' time, sheltered and supported a family of twelve,— how, only those who know how far toilsome thrift, and proud, independent effort, and simple, contented living can make scanty resources go, can best tell you. Seven of the ten children, with father and mother, slept now in the little graveyard that lay in the valley between the meeting-house and the broad, blue river. Only Lois and Lucretia, with a sister who years before had married David Romney, a farmer-neighbor, were left. They were, small, brown-haired, pleasant-faced women, so much alike that strangers ventured on no more distinctive title, in addressing them, than the impersonal Miss Fields. But others, better acquainted, knew that Miss Lois was the smaller, livelier, sharper-tongued of the trim, alert, kindly old-fashioned little ladies, who were so capable, who "managed" the big farm so successfully, and always seemed so independent and comfortable, driving to church in town, four miles away, every pleasant Sunday, and to the same busy little city two or three times in the week, with butter, eggs, or fruit, and to buy groceries; and occasionally making ready for an afternoon, making calls, or going to spend the day with friends in town or on a not too distant farm. Busy, kindly, cheery people they were,—with faces so true, so quiet and gentle, so serene and trustful, that you would hardly guess how sorely wrung with grief, how deeply plowed with sorrow, had been the hearts and the years behind them,—

though the blue eyes were deep-set, dimmed, and faded with tears shed long ago.

One of their "ways" was this morning reading,—always a chapter,—nearly always read in course. To-day it was the last chapter of First Timothy, and Miss Lucretia, whose turn it was to read, went back, after she had finished, to read again the seventeenth and eighteenth verses: "Charge them . . . that they do good, that they be rich in good works, ready to distribute, willing to communicate."

"Ready to distribute," she repeated. "I always liked the sound of that verse, though I never knew as I rightly understood what it means."

"Why, what it says, of course!"

"But how is anybody going to do it; and is it,—*ain't* it meant for us?"

"We aren't rich, by any means," rejoined Miss Lois, briskly; "and 'twas them that are rich he was talking about. But I suppose he *meant* every one, *accordingly*. And we do it, some."

"Yes, but we don't distribute but little, for folks that has so much all to themselves."

"We don't have a great sight, only the butter and eggs, and the hay and apples to sell, the farm is so run out,—unless David cuts some of the wood from the back lot, or we take summer boarders,—from which may we be delivered hereafter, if they're all like Liab Thorn's folks,—veritable *thorns*, and aggravating ones, they was. Though we do earn some spending-money tailoring."

"But we've done pretty well this year, what with the orchard doing so well, bearing an off-year, when apples are high; and the poultry and the butter; and Mis' Thorn paid pretty well, after all. And it's Thanksgiving time, and we've got fixed up so comfortable for winter, it don't seem right to just sit down and enjoy it all ourselves, and not give around any of it, when there's so many poor and discouraged and sorrowful and lonesome folks."

"Who are they, and what shall we give 'em?" inquired Miss Lois, attacking with her skimmer the yellow cream on the pans,—they were in the kitchen now,—while her sister cleared away the breakfast-table. "I'm willing. Only we'd better be about it; it's Tuesday now."

"Well," said Miss Lucretia, "there's Mrs. Leigh and Alice: They probably can't buy much for Thanksgiving, and wouldn't have time to cook it if they could. I'll carry them

a couple of my pies, a mince and a pumpkin,
I think."

"And we'll take 'em a chicken and some
greenings. Glad you thought of it. And
wouldn't it be a good plan to send a chicken
to Hannah Ham? We can spare two, I
guess."

"Yes, and a pie ; and Uncle Day must have
a pie and a loaf of bread and some doughnuts.
And, Lois, we shan't go anywhere to dinner,
—they'll ask us over to David's, David and
Ruth, but I know David's brothers are coming, and we don't want to go. And we could
invite one or two in just as well as not,
couldn't we?"

"Why, Lucretia Ann Fields, who do you
want to ask? The governor, or old Aunt
Sally Hawkes?"

"Why," answered Miss Lucretia, meekly
and hesitatingly, "I only thought there was
room enough, and everything so nice and
cheerful, with the rooms new-papered and
whitewashed this fall, and there's Mary
Elliott, Mrs. Emery, I mean, with her girl
and boy alone in that big house, feelin' so
proud and sad and lonesome since their father
disgraced all and then died and left 'em"—

"They wouldn't come here! I asked you
why you don't ask in the governor!"

"They would come, I b'lieve; and 'twould do Mary good, and the children, too, to get out here and look over to where she used to live when she was young,—where she grew up."

"We can't fix things nice enough for them."

"Yes, we can; they'll like the change."

"Well," replied Miss Lois emphatically, "if that's the plan, I'll hurry and get my hands out of the churning, and help you with the pies and doughnuts. I'll 'tend to the punkin. When did you think of inviting them?"

"We've got to carry in the butter to-morrow; that'll be time enough. When I carried the apples she ordered last week, I heard her say they was to be at home; she looked all overcome when the man who brings her things was asking if she wanted a turkey for Thanksgiving. She didn't seem to want to do anything the way she used to, but I surmised she thought she'd best make things as cheerful as she could for Anna and Allan. And we can take the things to Mrs. Leigh as we go along."

"How'll the Emerys get out here? They haven't got any horse, have they? And there's three of 'em, Anna and Allan, besides their mother."

"I thought," Miss Lucretia made answer, somewhat loth now to tell the plans she had

been revolving, and lead the campaign she
had so courageously begun,—"that Allan
could ride out on the milk wagon with Davy,
Thursday morning early, and take our team
and go in and bring his mother and Anna
out."

"And one of us can carry them home. Allan
can get a ride, maybe, some way. I wonder,
Lucretia, if one of our punkins, and maybe,
a few vegetables wouldn't come handy at the
Lowden's for Thanksgiving? We use sech a
few, ourselves, and thinkin' of them pies made
me think of it. There, the butter's done, and
now I'll carry it down cellar, and come right
off and help fill the pies."

So Lucretia mixed and rolled and flaked
and baked, and Miss Lois sifted and stirred
and sweetened and spiced, and at the early
sunset the speckless pantry shelves held rows
of tempting, toothsome Thanksgiving pies,
— pumpkin and squash, mince and apple,
cranberry and custard. A half dozen loaves
of bread, browned to perfection, were tilted
up to cool on the broad shelf by the window;
beside them stood a pan of doughnuts, spicy
and substantial; and Miss Lucretia was hand-
ling with care the cake, sponge and marble
and fruit cake, guiltless of frosting or icing or

meringue, yet wholesome and flavorous, as well as fragrant.

"Now, Lucretia, you're just clean tired out!" exclaimed Lois, as she took down her milk pails. "You just go lie down while I do the chores. I'll put the teakettle on, and when I come in I'll make the tea, and put on the supper. You're all beat out."

But bright and early next morning, their capacious wagon filled, back and front, with bags and baskets and two or three enormous yellow pumpkins,—the sisters started townward. Their load grew rapidly less as they entered and rode along the streets of the city, though the unusual celerity with which their neighborly errands were done,—a haste remarkable in the usually sociable Lois, cut short or averted altogether the thanks of the half-dozen women, each of whom was in her own way surprised, touched, gratified, grateful for the unlooked for kindness, and the unexpected accession to her store. Mrs. Leigh regretfully rose from her sewing,— moments were precious with her, and her day's work hard to be accomplished,—as they stopped at her door. But her thankfulness and wonderment were evident, though only half-uttered. And, if the donors could have heard her thoughts and known that their current was turned from despondent anxiety to a happier mood by their benefaction, they would have felt themselves richly repaid.

"We *can* keep Thanksgiving, after all. I couldn't spare the money to buy anything, nor take any time to-day even to cook. But now I can finish this job to-day, and that will make out money enough to pay for a ton of coal. Mollie has the day to-morrow out of the store, and we can get that chicken into the oven, and the vegetables ready, and we can go to church. And I will take two or three of those big apples Miss Fields brought, for a bit of sauce, and cut a couple of pieces out of the pumpkin pie, for our supper. That'll leave more than enough for to-morrow, with the mince. And the best of it is, it makes a body feel that *God does care.* We might be so much worse off! Yes, we've a good deal to be thankful for, every way. We've got friends, and we've got God, and *they* make one feel surer of *him.*"

It was with more trepidation that Lucretia entered Mrs. Emery's sitting-room. She had had butter and eggs to bring, which, being old acquaintances, the sisters had furnished before and since their friend's sorrows,—and this gave her an errand. But her embassy was soon accomplished.

"Well," said Lois, "will they come? I 'spose they *will*,—you look like it. And what's that you've got in your hand, Lucretia?"

"Yes, indeed; Mary seemed real pleased to think we thought of it, and I think she was glad to get out on the Hill again, in sight of the old place. She said they wasn't going anywhere else, and wasn't going to do much at home, and she went up and asked Anna, and Anna came down, too. And they both said it would be a real delight to 'em, and they was very grateful for our remembrance of 'em. And this book I was a-looking at while Mary was out of the room,—Lucy Larcom's poems; you know I've cut her pieces out of the Transcript a good many times. And Anna Emery, she would have me take it home to read; and she's got other books she said we might have; Mrs. Whitney's, and somebody she called Miss Jewett, and the woman that wrote 'The Gates Ajar.' And books of poetry, and sermons, too. She showed me some of 'em, and she said she should bring out some Thursday. 'Twill be a real God-send this winter. And they both seemed as pleased and friendly as could be. They said Allan would be tickled to come. And I shouldn't wonder, Lois, if we should get considerable well acquainted and sociable with 'em, if things go well. Somehow there's quite a number of folks seem a sight nearer than they did last week."

"Maybe so, maybe so. Hurry up, Jack! Tom Harriman'll be round after them chickens before we get home, I'm afeard. Don't know what he'll say at our keeping out so many, after they was all dressed for the store, too. Catch him a-givin' away one! for all he's worth his clear ten thousand, *and* the farm."

Tom Harriman, drover and butcher, as well as farmer,—tight-fisted, as he must needs have been, to lay up a competency on those bleak Maine hills, drove up to their door just as Lois and Lucretia, the one having unharnessed, while the other unlocked the house and stirred up the fire,—were laying away their wraps and the now empty baskets. A little surprised at the lessened store of poultry awaiting him, he soon surmised, though he said no word, the cause of its depletion, and, unknown to the sisters, was moved to two or three generous donations to less prosperous neighbors, in honor of the season, and to a liberality in "bartering," weighing, and making change, that was quite unusual to him. And as he went on his way over the rocky roads, past the fields where the after-math was brown, and the bloom of the golden-rod, lately so bonny, clung, frost-burnt and faded, to its withering stalk,—while his maiden neighbors were taking down their quaint, precious china, straining their cranberry jelly, dusting and garnishing their low, pleasant, old-fashioned rooms,—he was somehow reminded how soon the busiest, most prosperous, longest life is done ; how little of his hardly-gotten gains could be carried into that low house where the western sun gleamed bright on the old, white, slanting stones,—how little, alas ! he had so spent that he could well carry the investment on into the lofty mansions beyond,—the Father's house ; how many opportunities there were, even now, of doing and giving ; and what a warm feeling was somehow at one's heart when one *had* reached out a generous, helping hand.

Once more the November sunshine—this time from a tender, cloudless sky, such as the vanishing Autumn sometimes gives us as she passes—looked in on the busy, expectant sisters in the old farmhouse, making their final preparations for the Thanksgiving feast, to grace which a huge, plump turkey was already steaming in the oven.

Very swiftly this Thanksgiving sun seemed to climb the stainless blue, smiling, at ten o'clock, on the arriving guests; beaming on the quiet, yet heartily enjoyed "visiting" that filled the remaining forenoon; and resting, with a benignity that was a benediction, on the little group around the great, square table, decked with glass and china, fruit and flowers, and burdened with its Thanksgiving cheer; on the guests, not beguiled into forgetfulness of their sorrows, but reminded of the Father, who "ordereth all things after the counsel of his will;" whose "tender mercies are over all his works;" whose love, both his giving and withholding shall prove and unfold; on whose errands, in paths of service, and in ministries to other lives, the weakest and poorest may be going; and on the silvering hair of our friends, the sisters, Lois and Lucretia,—thankful in their joys, trustful in their silent griefs, and loneliness, and glad, with a new gladness, in "distributing" the Lord's bounty.

AN OLD SONG.

The mellow October sunshine lay warm on stony hill and dusty intervale, as, between the bordering maples, scarlet and golden in their early autumn glory, Mrs. Ada Shirley rode in her easy carriage, her thoughts busy with certain secret, well-premeditated · unmalevolent designs. "This sunlight is lovely, but moonlight is. irresistible," she soliloquized. "No man in his right mind, and in love, can stand that. And the moon fulls to-morrow, and next day's Thursday—*my* day." But her musings were interrupted here, for turning the lane to the Ray farm, she overtook the object of her quest, and indirectly of her meditations, sauntering leisurely up the grassy road, her hands full of gay autumn leaves, and fading golden-rod, and over-ripe and plumy grasses.

"Why, it's you, is it Ada, and you're coming to see me? How delightful!"

"Yes, it's I," responded Mrs. Ada. "Jump in, Helen. It's you I wanted to see, and I can't stay long. You see," she resumed, a moment later, "I'm going to have a tea-party to improve this lovely weather. You must be there, of course, and I want you to come out in the morning and stay over night. You will, won't you? Thursday night it's going to be—just a little company—the minister and his wife, and Ned and Grace Waylin, and Nettie Robson and Joe, and two or three others."

"Why, yes, I suppose I can come. That is, if mother has no objections. I don't know of any reason why I can't be spared."

"Spared! Of course you can be spared! You're not half so necessary as you think yourself," was her companion's rejoinder, as she tied her gray horse to the farmer's gate-post.

Whether her assertions were true or not, it transpired that Miss Helen could very well be spared on this occasion, and the mother, whose steadfast, brown eyes might have passed for Helen's own, so alike they were, promised that she should be at the village bright and early Thursday morning.

"Did you know John Loring was at home?" asked Mrs. Shirley, as, her errand done, they lingered on the little piazza overhung with scarlet creepers, to chat of neighborhood news. "But of course you did, you'd have seen him at church."

The gray horse was impatient, and his mistress was even then in the carriage, and a moment afterward off. An hour later she was saying to her husband, "She's coming, and she knew John was here, though I didn't give her a chance to ask if he was coming, too. Thursday night she saw him at church, she said. I can't make out whether it was anything more than a friendly meeting, but I guess that was all. And I don't know as there *is* anything; and I don't know *but* there is. Anyway, I'm going to give 'em a chance to find out. I know John Loring and Helen Ray thought they belonged to each other once, for good and all. And I know something's come between 'em, but I don't know what."

Something *had* come between. Mrs. Shirley had stated the case correctly, both as regarded the past and present status of the two persons she was interested in. Ten years before, John Loring, fresh from college and after-training, had returned to his native town, ready to put out his sign with the "M. D." he had been earning, affixed to his name, and to settle among his kindred and townsmen in the prosecution of his calling. And he had hoped, too, that about the time he should hang out the aforesaid sign with its fresh lettering, a certain little brown house on a sunny corner might receive the village doctor and his bride as tenants. He and Helen Ray *had* belonged to each other, by mutual, tacit understanding; and it was full of inexplicable pain and mystery to our young physician that in resolute disregard of this unwritten bond, Helen should, at this time have withdrawn herself so completely, with such unmistakable intention of avoidance and refusal, from engagement, intimacy, friendship. He could not even gain opportunity to beg for explanation, though, indeed, it was doubtful if she would have unfolded her reasons. All the hope, and promise, and even the sheltering, her girlhood had known seemed to fail Helen Ray. The farm was mortgaged, and, unless something were done, would soon pass out of their hands altogether. Her father was despondent and discouraged, her mother was ill, her brother and sister young and dependent. There was only Helen to summon and concentrate the few and scattering energies of the household ; only she to care for the mother and cheer and advise the father, and keep the house, and strive to make the payments, and insist on opportunity of renewals; only she, either to earn a dollar aside from the products of the farm; only she to maintain that the younger daughter and the son should have something like suitable preparation for the tug their hands must lay hold on by and by. And all these things, and more than these, she had done. She had upheld her father's courage and incited him to close and profitable cultivation of their incumbered acres. By unremitting care and insistence on every benefit of treatment and comfort, she had won her mother back to health. She had looked after and sent to the best market every product that came within her province. She had done fine sewing between whiles, for old friends in town, not to speak of the other interminable stitches she had set in garments that were not "fine," for the homefolks. For it was she who cut and turned and sponged and pressed, and altered and fitted and draped, in that not unimportant part of the struggle that lay in the region of "keeping up appearances." And, after a little, she had gathered a music class, and with the help of her beloved piano, secured in more prosperous years, had added not a little to the family income. And she had not laid down her oars till the tide had fairly turned. And when it had turned it came in with a rush, and bore the little craft of the family fortune steadily towards prosperity. The farm began to yield a revenue, and now was sure of giving them a comfortable living. The "children" were well established, May as teacher in a neighboring academy, Fred as foreman in a large manufactory not far distant. And when there remained but one small payment to make the farm theirs, a legacy, that seemed to them now quite a little fortune, came to them, and filled the measure of their content and competence.

Helen had felt that she could not hint to John Loring the reason of her reserve. She could not have asked him even to "bide a wee" for her sake, for it was likely to be a long struggle. "It might be for years, and it might be forever." And whether he had ever known, or heard of their adversities, she did not know. He had changed his mind about settling in his native Clayton. She had meant him to keep at a distance, and he straightway put well-nigh the breadth of the continent between them; and, having won standing and the beginnings of success in his profession, he had come back to Clayton for an October's vacation; if for any other object, not even the gossips knew nor could surmise it.

"Perhaps Helen Ray could tell," suggested one of them, tentatively to another.

"Nell Ray!" returned Jennie Austin, in fine scorn. "Why, she doesn't even correspond with him, and hasn't, at all! She's as ignorant as the rest, you may rest assured."

And, of course, the advent of this young physician, with the possibility, real or conjectured, that he might settle in Clayton, made some stir socially in the town.

"All the girls are after him," observed Mrs. Shirley, to her husband.

"And some one of them will be pretty sure to get him, unless he's otherwise engaged," returned he.

"I'm afraid so," sighed the wife. "Men have so little discernment! The idea of a man looking the second time at that shallow little Anna Arden, or Marie Nelson, or Eva Manton, when there's my splendid Helen Ray! Only *she* isn't in the market, and never will be. Well, I'll try my tea-party and the harvest-moon."

At which her husband only smiled, but not so slightingly as if he had not had previous

4

experience of his wife's insight, and her ability to make the simplest means further her pur-poses.

And so the looked for Thursday came, arched by skies as serene as ever shed October sunlight. .The two friends, matron and maid, had been together all day, making the pretty little home gay with autumn spoils, and assisted by the admiring Shirley twins, Jack and Alice. A pleasant day they had had. "The best part of your party, I know, Ada," said Helen, half laughing, half in earnest. "I wish you'd let me go home now!"

" Go home now, indeed! No, ma'am! And how do you know what's the best of it, I wonder? 'The best is yet to be,—the last of life for which the first was made,' as the husband of your favorite, Mrs. Browning, sings," replied blithe, little Mrs. Shirley, as she surveyed with complacency her festive tea table.

 And, indeed, it was a very charming little tea. The *bouillon* was perfect, the sandwiches irreproachable, the rolls were like feathers for lightness and like snow for whiteness; the jellies and preserves had the ripe, new flavor such confections, newly made, ought to have, and the coffee was golden and fragrant, and the cake was a marvellous compound of sweetness and light. And it was a pleasant and congenial company, also. They had all been schoolmates, and some of them classmates, in their not far distant youth, clergymen and all. And the harvest moon was shining in all its serenity and glory, when they rose from the table. There was only one drawback, if drawback it was.

"Miss Harris has sent me a note," whispered Helen to their hostess as they went to the parlors. "She wants me to stay with her to-night. I'm sorry, but I'll just slip out early, and 'twon't make any difference. Jack can go over with me, can't he?"

"Miss Harris? O, Helen, what a pity! Of course, Jack can go, but you can't go *very* early. Why I depended on your music, you know."

But the quiet little lady in golden brown, careless of the magic that slept in voice and fingers, was even quieter than usual that evening, and for an hour or two engaged herself with the clergyman's wife, in a nook equally remote from the piano and from Dr. Loring, who had not failed to be there, and who, it should be said, had been pressed into service as the messenger of Miss Harris, an invalid friend in the village.

But his blue eyes were keener than of old. He had not been watching signs and symptoms for ten years for nothing; and he knew how to put this and that together, too, if he was a man. He had found out already, that the evident prosperity the Rays were now enjoying had succeeded a period of trial and privation; that Helen had had her share in the family stress and strain, and had lavished her young strength and her first youth in redeeming the family fortunes. Of the long illness that succeeded when her tense hold of the oars began to slacken, he knew, too, and her music, and herself, as woman, daughter, sister, friend. And he could see, under the disguises of the evening's excitement, the dainty dress, and the quiet dignity and cheerfulness, that shadows were around the brown eyes, and that the eyes themselves were deeper and stiller; that the hands were thin, not only, but roughened and marred; that the slight form was bent a trifle, and the wrists had been distended with something beside piano-practice. And how very still she was, yet how bright and thoughtful when she did speak! These had not been idle years for her, nor unfruitful ones.

The little group at the piano was dissolving, and Alice Shirley, admitted for the first time to a "grown-up party," came to beg Helen to sing.

"Not to-night, Allie," she answered ; then as there arose a pleading murmur from other lips, she could no longer refuse. Two or three brilliant pieces she played, and sang one or two simple songs, and was about to rise, when Alice placed before her another sheet, begging her to "sing just this, Miss Helen, that you sang for me the other day, and I won't ask for another."

Any other selection from Ada's music rack or her own overflowing stores would have been easier. She hesitated a moment, then divining that she could only escape by yielding, sang, with exquisite simplicity, yet with feeling and pathos she could not conceal, the old, familiar song :—

> "The puir auld folk at home, ye mind,
>   Are frail and failing sair,
>   And well I ken they'd miss me, lad,
>   Gin I came hame nae mair;
> The grist is out, the times are hard, the kine are only three;
>   I canna leave the auld folk now,
>   We'd better bide a wee;
>   I canna leave the auld folk now,
>   We'd better bide a wee."

The three verses of the song she sang, straight through, with slight and softly-mingled prelude and accompanying chords, constrained, in part, at least, by the hush that fell on the little company, and the rapt attention they gave. And it was easy, in the little stir of freer movement and appreciative praise, to slip out then, don wraps and beckon to Ada.

"Yes, dear, I really must go now. Miss Harris will be looking for me. Where's Jack? Or, never mind about the boy, I'm not a bit afraid, such moonlight as it is!"

But a deeper voice answered her, "Here is an older Jack at your service, if he will do, or if you will let him try. I promised Miss Harris I would see you safely there."

And so, amazed, but thrilling with a prophetic sense of triumph exceeding her wildest schemes for the evening, the little hostess saw them go out into the moonlight, and went back to her guests with satisfied heart.

"What a marvellous moon!" the lady ventured to remark, when a few steps had been taken in silence. But as the only reply she got was an absent, "Yes, very," she resigned herself to silence the remainder of their walk.

It was, indeed, a marvellous moon. It flooded the familiar street with its serene brightness, and photographed on dusty street and pavement each leaf and twig of the overarching trees. There was a warmth in it, as of sunlight twice refined, and fragrance, too, akin to that distilled in the dews of summer twilight; only, where that is of flowers, this was of fruits. And though the hoar-frost was beginning to show its silvery rime here and there, and the flower-beds on either hand had their nocturnal coverings of cast-off wraps and ghostly newspapers, and sable waterproofs, to protect from its blackening touches, it was not chilly.

All these things Helen had had time to observe, when her companion broke out in earnest, impetuous speech,—

"I've been a fool, Helen. It's been growing upon me this long while, that I'd behaved like an idiot; but now I am sure of it. And since you sang that song to-night, I can't help asking you if *that* was the reason you turned so cold all at once ten years ago? I was so hurt and dazed at first, I didn't think of anything like that; and I went off, and 'twas too late. But that *was it*, wasn't it? And we *will* set it right, now, sha'n't we?"

And to this ambiguous and chaotic declaration, Helen could only answer faintly, .

"Oh! John!"

But John seemed satisfied, and it was well the moonlight could not photograph sound, for earnest talk went on all the way to the

Harris gate, and under the elms at the gateway, till the sound of voices in the distance warned them that Mrs. Shirley's tea-party was over. And when in ecstatic satisfaction, she heard of its result, and knew that the young doctor had entered into partnership with old Dr. Small, well on in years, and ready to relinquish all save office work; and that the young physician would install his bride as mistress of the cozy brown house opposite her own home, she only said to her husband, as rejoiced as she,—

"It was that moonlight, and I *knew* it would do it!"

But she did not know, though either of the two interested parties could have told her,— for they hold the fact in tender remembrance, —that the chief hastening cause was only an old song.

DEACON LANE'S STRAWBERRY BED.

It was his by purchase only, and there were
certain conditions attaching thereto. It had
been prepared and tended by his neighbor,
Deacon Johnson. They lived on a high hill
just out of Edgarly, difficult of access, yet
commanding a wide and inspiring view. The
fertile, closely-tilled acres of Deacon Johnson's
little farm adjoined Deacon Lane's broad fields
and valuable woodlands, stretching away from
either side of the long, travelled road. Here,
Jerome Johnson had passed two decades of his
tranquil life. His cheery, little wife had shared
his affectionate tendance of shrub and tree and
vine and flower, and made the one-storied cottage a radiant centre of peace, hospitality, and
a thousand beneficent ministries, for years.
But she had faded out of life, like one of her
own blossoms. Since then the lonely husband
had found his best comfort, next to the conso-

lations of the Divine Comforter, which his friends well knew, were staff and strength and stay, in the places where something of her presence seemed still to linger. He loved to walk in the garden she had planned, the growing orchard they had planted together, and especially to maintain her modest, though abundant, accustomed charities.

But perhaps the good man missed her care more than her roses and raspberries did, for one winter, when the snow had lain on the windy Long Hill for months, his always delicate health gave way. He must leave the North at once, the physician said. Only a Southern home could hold him on earth, if indeed he might linger longer in any human habitation. Only his out-door life through the summer months of years, and his diligent, generous tranquility, had prolonged his life thus far.

So the gentle, lonely man, still serene and untroubled for himself, made his preparations for a journey to Florida. It was hard parting with his home, but he could never live again in the North, so his few, fruitful acres passed into his neighbor's hands. It was late in February when the deed was made out. And on the day of his departure, Deacon Lane brought the transfer-papers for him to sign, though the bargain had not yet been concluded.

"There is one thing, Brother Lane," began the invalid, as he slowly unfolded the papers awaiting his sanction and signature, "that I meant to have spoken to you about; my largest plat of strawberries, you know, is just coming into full bearing this year. There's a full acre of it. I've given it the best of care, and it will doubtless yield, with very little attention, a very profitable crop."

His listener's eyes brightened at the gainful prospect.

"Of course, Brother Johnson, I'm willing to pay you what's right. We can't count on crops that are under eight feet of solid snow, but I'm willing to make fair allowance."

The contrast between the friends, for friends they were, and equally staunch, was striking. Deacon Lane was short, wiry, and muscular, with a sharp, sallow face, and restless, despondent gray eyes. He sat leaning forward in his chair, his fingers moving nervously. Real sorrow and anxious pity seemed queerly blended, in his countenance and attitude, with the keen calculation and satisfied complacency attendant on the bargain about to be consummated.

Deacon Jerome was a tall man, of massive frame, ere sickness had wasted it. His face was as white as his snowy hair; he leaned back in his arm-chair, his deep blue eyes bent in benignant reflection alternately on his neighbor and on the unfolded deeds his own thin hands held.

"I don't think I shall add anything to the sum we talked of," he said, at last, slowly; "but there are one or two conditions—"

"You'd ought to have told me, Deacon," put in Mr. Lane, quickly, "before the papers were all drawn up."

But the other lifted his hand deprecatingly. "No, I don't care to have them in the bond, Brother," he said, smilingly. "Your word is enough. It is only this: there are a few sick folk to whom I should carry some of my berries. I don't want them to lose their share. So, if you will promise to carry them their portion, I will call myself paid."

So, with visible surprise and secret reluctance, Deacon Lane promised. The deeds were signed, and the money paid. And that night he saw his great-hearted neighbor on board the train, looked after his comfort with clumsy kindness, and wrung his hand at parting with sincere sorrow.

And then other interests crowded out the thought of the snow-bound and not unincumbered strawberry-bed. But ere long the snows

wasted, and when the protecting "brush" was
removed, the fresh, vigorous growth of vine
appeared right queenly. The blossoms opened,
faded, and fell, and the new, green berries
began to form or "set."   Day by day he
watched his strawberries slowly swelling and
reddening in the sweet fierce sun and shower,
and he began to remember his promise.   It had
dawned upon his recollection, that February
night, ere the southern-bound train had gone
a hundred inches, that he had promised (Oh,
Deacon Johnson, benignantly crafty!) to go
in person, carrying his gifts.

The Lane household was a severely still and
solemn one. Practically, it was a childless
home. The gentleness and self-devotion of
the mother had so far failed to counteract or
compensate for the father's sternness that the
children had early escaped its doubtful comforts. The eldest and staidest had entered a
village store, and soon had a business and a
home of his own. The second, Theodore,
"took to books." But he got scant aid, opportunity, or encouragement, and left home in
boyhood to work his way through academy
and college. Though still young, he had now
a professorship in a neighboring city. The
only daughter, Annie, died in girlhood.

June had waxed and was waning when the berries ripened, maturing slowly. The clusters hung, however, full and heavy on the rank, vigorous vines, which had missed the training and pruning of their former owner. But Deacon Lane watched vine and runner complacently, picking his way among the straying off-shoots, turning the bunches, hiding here and there, to the sun. He had two or three times picked a bowlful for tea; and he discovered that nothing that had ever graced his little breakfast-table had had so rare, wholesome, delicious a flavor, and so inviting a semblance, as a dish of those same, dewy strawberries. He began to wonder why he had never had any before.

"They help my liver, I do believe!" murmured the querulous, dyspeptic man, in whose dietary the three P's—Pork, Potatoes, Pie,—had been the principal features.

It was almost time to market the berries; and he began to think it would be, as it were, placating fortune to carry first some of his strawberries to the sick ones. From the list his friend had given him, he chose the name of Eben Clark; and one bright morning, a little basket of berries in his hand, he started out.

Eben Clark was ninety, and bed-ridden. He and his feeble wife lived with their son, Jonathan, half way down Long Hill. It was years since the Deacon had entered their dwelling, or, indeed, as Brother Johnson well knew, any of the homes these names represented. Yet they were those of friends, neighbors, brethren. But he often looked longingly toward this one. Jonathan Clark owed him a long-standing debt. It was not a large one, but enough to make his creditor sigh for its payment, and notice grudgingly anything like prosperity or self-indulgence on the part of the debtor.

It was a small, weather-beaten house, on the edge of sloping, sterile acres. Everything about it proclaimed neatness and economy. Mrs. Clark, the younger, answered his knock.

"Oh! it is Deacon Lane, I declare, with some berries for Gran'ther. Come in and see him while I empty the basket. Indeed, you must," as he hesitated; "he's so childish he'd never get over it if you didn't. Jonathan's a-workin' at the querry, but Grandma'am, she's here."

So the Deacon followed her into a low-ceiled room, with whitewashed walls and rag-carpeted floor. A frail old lady sat knitting by the

window; and propped up by pillows on the
great, high-posted bed was Gran'ther Clark.
His gnarled, brown hands, tortured and twisted
with rheumatism, were folded on the coarse,
white, knitted coverlet. The Deacon shook
hands and sat down, and the old man began to
talk feebly, of his pains, his pleasures, "his
folks :"

"I *have* suffered consider'ble this winter;
and I can't help myself yet, much. An' Mary
here, is 'most too frail to move me. But Jonathan, now, can lift me like a baby. Dretful
good to me, Jonathan is, an' always has been.
We've been a heavy load for him to lug; but
he says, says he, 'Father, I don't want you
ever to say *that* agin. You've toted me when
I couldn't help myself, and never begredged
it.' An' Jonathan's never begredged *us* anything; an' I'm in hopes 'twon't be much longer,
now—not much longer! Well Deacon," he
resumed, not noticing the other's silence, "it
seems good to hev you come in. We miss
Mr. Johnson a sight. An' you must pray
with us afore ye go. I used to hear ye to
prayer-meetin' years ago."

Isaac Lane had not come there to pray, but
he could not refuse; but, somehow, as he
knelt, his reserve and his grudging thoughts

melted away. And when he finished, the old man added his hearty, tremulous "Amen!" and Grandma Clark wiped her eyes and thanked him. He took himself away very hastily then ; and he tried to forget all about it straightway, but somehow he was not content till he had dropped into the Post Office, enclosed in an envelope addressed to ".J. Clark, Esq.," that old bill receipted.

The next name was Mrs. Nathan True. She was the invalid wife of a former "hand" of the Deacon's. He had left the mill to the lasting inconvenience and annoyance of his employer, because he wanted, needed, must have, he said, higher wages. A large tin pail, heaping full, the owner of the strawberry-bed carried this time, as he approached Nathan True's open door. It was Nathan himself, just home from work, and preparing for supper, who welcomed him.

"How are you, Deacon ! Glad to see you. Come in, come in !" and he led the way into the middle room, where the eldest daughter had already his supper ready. Coarse and simple the food was, yet neat and inviting. The visitor found himself counting the children already around the table. One, two, three, four, five, six, yes, and that youngest in the high chair made seven, besides the young housekeeper. All those mouths Nathan True must feed! No wonder things showed that every dollar and cent must yield its full value.

"Mr. Lane's brought mother some strawberries," said the father. "Lucy, you put them away, or p'raps she'd like to see 'em. And, Fred, run and ask her if she feels able to see an old friend a minute."

And once more our friend found himself in a sick room. A pale, wan woman, apparently suffering with incurable disease, sat in a pillowed chair. Her eyes were bright, and her smile sweet. A workbasket, heaped with children's worn clothing, stood near her, and a thimble was on one thin finger. Mrs. True was a sister in the church, and it required no effort on the Deacon's part to be genial and kindly, hiding as well as he could his shocked surprise at the ravages of sickness.

He did not stay long. Once more he had something to think of. And the thought would not be laid, though he tried to content himself with urging Mrs. Lane to carry comforts and delicacies to "Nate True's sick wife," himself driving her over in an easy carriage. It did not satisfy him either, though it surprised

Mrs. Lane, to insist on less work, more leisure, more abundant comfort everyway for his own meek wife. A week or two later, he offered Nathan True his old place in the mill, and higher pay than the employé had asked. And he was ready, too, to pay more generous wages to other men. He had seen for himself how one workman lived; and he knew that in one instance, at least, it was neither laziness nor extravagance that gauged the measure of "living wages."

In the meantime, the Deacon had been checking off, one by one, the names on his list. He had made a half dozen unwilling, though not unenjoyable, calls. None of them had produced any striking results, yet none had been wholly unproductive of gracious influences.

Now only one name remained—Elizabeth Allen. It was not the name of an aged person, a widow, or a bed-ridden woman. She did not even call herself an invalid. A fall, eight years before, had made it impossible for her to walk or stand. She was not a typical submissive sufferer. It was, indeed, hope, rather than resignation, that sustained her, though it was still hope deferred. There was the very confident assurance of an able physician that treatment at a certain distant and famous hospital would cure her. But the money was not forthcoming, though they were by no means poor. Twice, what her fingers had earned and hoarded, had been given to meet some emergency of sickness or family trouble, and now her little earnings were growing slowly again. Deacon Lane dreaded this call most of all. His reluctance would have been difficult to explain, for Jonathan Allen had been an old friend; the families once were intimate, and Elizabeth had been the dear friend of his own Annie. But little misunderstandings and jealousies had grown into positive estrangement. And it did not soften the Deacon's resentful obduracy to know that Theodore, during his infrequent visits home, always went there; nay, had even been known to drive over to the Allens of an evening or holiday when he did not stop at his father's.

It was ten o'clock in the forenoon, and the men were in the field, when Deacon Lane rode over. Mrs. Allen was baking in the kitchen, and with a brief, though cordial, greeting— her bread was burning—ushered him with his basket into the cool sitting-room where Elizabeth sat, busied with her needle-work. Always dignified and at ease of yore, he wondered why the young lady should flush and start as he entered. Nor was it quite easy to maintain a conversation. But she soon recovered herself and talked as brightly as of old.

As he went nearer to examine the dainty, beautifully-shaded work she wished him to see, he saw, lying in her work-basket, a letter, directed to herself, its seal just broken. It was a thick letter, and the Deacon was confident that it was addressed in his son Theodore's peculiar hand. Like a stream of light the circumstance illumined a thousand unheeded happenings,—unnoticed in his own hard, selfish reserve. The embroidery on which she was working, the prospect of cure of which she spoke so hopefully, the letter there, the remembered visits,—yes, and the long, long years of waiting!

Ah! did he know less of his boy's heart and hope, of his love and pains, than strangers did? Had he been so busy heaping up that he had forgotten to use? Were real estate, and bank stock, and moneyed capital, so much more precious than love and life? He had been blind! But it was not too late, even now, and he saw!

Again that day, at sunset, while Farmer Allen stood in his wide barn-door, Deacon

Lane drove over the cross-road and up the grassy lane. He did not go to the house; his business, he thought, was better done with the father, and it was more easily accomplished than he had feared.

"I won't deny it has been hard, Deacon," said the farmer; "hard for us, and harder for Elizabeth, but she never complains nor loses heart. Doctor Bell is certain she can be made to walk as well as anybody if she can go to the hospital. I may as well tell you, she won't, that she's had half enough, or more, twice. The first time, her mother was sick, and she used it for that. Then a note I'd signed came back on me, and she helped me out with that. And, perhaps you don't know it, but since Theodore has had his professorship, *he* wanted to pay for her to go and be treated, but she wouldn't let him. I haven't told her, but I've been in hopes, when my crops come in, I could give her enough, with what she's got. I'm a-planning for it."

But Deacon Lane had a plan of his own. He had a will of his own, too, and it did not take long to convince the father and mother of the wisdom of *his* way. Elizabeth was harder to persuade, but she, too, was finally won over. Theodore was left in the dark for the present.

Before the last berry had shrunken on the strawberry vines, or the Deacon had had time to count his receipts, Elizabeth was on her way to the hospital. It was almost Thanksgiving time when she came back, her own active self. It was a happy party—a family party, the Deacon called it slyly, with a glance at Elizabeth, though all the Allens were there, as well as the Lanes—that gathered at the Deacon's on Thanksgiving day.

And before the strawberries. had ripened again, in early June, there was a wedding at Farmer Allen's, and Professor Theodore and his wife Elizabeth were domiciled for the summer in the vine-hung Johnson cottage.

'Deacon Lane still cultivates a strawberry-bed. He has had to re-set the old one, and has enlarged it. He thinks he has improved upon it in some respects. The berries are larger and seem of better flavor. Be that as it may, the fruits of his own Christian character are certainly more abundant and genial and mellow as the years go by.

A TARDY VALENTINE.

It was the mildest day of the season, and the fairest. So lovely, indeed, that it had already been named "a weather-breeder" several times in Pomfret, for the typical New Englander is always suspicious of unusual serenity, whether of fortune, manners, or the weather.

But the tender blue of the sky, now fast turning to amber in the light of the near sunset, was still almost cloudless. Against it the leafless oaks, the sturdy hemlocks and the darker evergreens on the wooded hills, stood out distinctly, while a group of white birches, very near the horizon, crossed the azure with strands of silver in a bit of dainty color that an artist would have coveted for his canvass.

But Mrs. Wills, who had sought her west attic room, to search through its well-assorted piece-bags, standing in a row, like so many very rotund and headless ghosts, hardly stopped to glance from the window that framed this February picture. The log-cabin quilt she was piecing lacked in one color.

"Too much grey for the scarlet, by half," she said, half aloud. "And I do believe I shall have to dye, unless I did save those red flannel petticoats. I'm sure I can't remember." .

The bags yielded their various stores, but to little purpose.

"One skirt—h'm—why, I gave the others to Jane Gunnison. I aint sorry, either, but I could feel to wish for a little more myself just now. Let me see! Why, there is that remnant of red flannel I bought so long ago. 'Twas a sizable piece, and I remember putting it in new camphor only last spring. And I'd just as lief use it."

The bags were tidily repacked, and Mrs. Wills crossed the room and opened a drawer in the antique mahogany bureau beside the window. The roll of flannel chanced to be at the back of the drawer, and two boxes, one of paste-board, time-stained and fragile, the other of oak, filled the nearer space. The deep drawer was full of shadows, and Mrs. Wills moved the lighter box injudiciously, so that it was presently aslant the drawer and wedged in.

5

A vigorous pull released it, and parted at the same time, lid from box and side from bottom, scattering its contents as she lifted it out, over all the adjacent floor. These consisted chiefly of old letters, very yellow as to paper and envelope—where they possessed the latter—and very much faded as to the ink, defining the precise, carefully formed words and letters. A few old-fashioned visiting cards were among them, and a photograph or two; also, a thin, small, oblong package, neatly wrapped in tissue paper, now gray with years. She had placed all the rest in the oaken box, discarding the other, when she picked up this.

She held it in her hand a minute, a shadow in her pleasant eyes, and a drooping, sorrowful curve taking its place among the finer lines around her firm, placid mouth, where the cares and trials of sixty years seemed to have been folded away snugly, that they might take to themselves just as little space and attention as possible, and then she sat down and opened the paper.

An ancient valentine, of the fashion of forty years before, fell out. It revealed now its original delicacy of coloring, and the paper outside the quaint, filagreed design was fine and glossy. A pink anchor sheltered a verse at once fond and tender, evidently the expression of friendship rather than love. On the inner leaf, in ruled spaces left for them, names had been written:

To

Lucinda Sinclair

from

Frances Bushfield,

and the date, February the fourteenth, 184—.

The envelope was unaddressed, and Mrs. Wills regarded both it and the valentine a long time intently.

"I ought to have sent it," she said, at last, regretfully, "and not minded what folks said. Maybe she didn't ever say what they said she did say. And, anyway, who knows what *they* said first to make her say it? She was having a good deal to try her, with Joe Barrett's going off that way, and her brother dying as he did, and I s'pose she hardly knew how she did feel for a while. And she must have needed a friend them days. I've always been disappointed in myself that I didn't stand by her, whether or no, through that; that was none of it her fault. She was the patientiest girl, and the nicest! I wished I'd sent it!

"And I don't wonder she was some distant to me afterwards. I'd a' been so myself, not knowing what reason I'd had to feel put out. She's been through a good deal since then, too, more than I have, though I've had my share. I wonder if she ever thinks of them old days, and our good times together? Why, there was nobody, scarcely, I set such store by as I did by her. And I used to think, 'Well, Lucy and I'll always be friends till we get to be old women.'

"And that was forty years ago, and we haven't crossed each other's threshold, except to funerals, and once or twice to a prayer-meeting that we couldn't stay away from on account of Christian feeling and example, in all that time.

"A willin',·true-hearted woman she's showed herself, and I guess very loving to them that was kin, though they're all gone now, husband and all, same as mine.

"But here I am talking about her as if she were dead and buried, and I saw her in her pew across the meeting-house only last Sabbath with a bonnet on that becomes her extra well.

"And my kitchen fire'll be out, and, land sakes, I forgot I'd just put on new coal to the other room grate !"

The carpeted stairs creaked as she somewhat stiffly descended them, and the warm air of the living rooms, fragrant with scents of geranium and heliotrope, was grateful after the chilly atmosphere of the chambers. The coal was ablaze, and the dampers had even to be closed by degrees. Then the kitchen fire was low and the cat was mewing on the window sill outside, begging to be taken in and petted. From that side of the house was plainly visible the home of her girlhood friend, the brown house under the elms, with sloping, red roofs, in which long-paned windows were set, and the great barns "to windward," making a prominent feature in the winter scene. The field between lay white and untrodden. It was only a little distance that way, though much farther if you followed the road. But the open door made the house chilly.

Pussy rubbed sociably against her mistress' foot, purring·loudly, and was consoled with a saucer of milk, "if it was between meals."

Then the sitting-room fire needed more attention, and as she turned to the window again, she saw a woman coming up the path.

"Lucretia Payne," said Mrs. Wills, putting up her hands to smooth her tumbled hair before the glass.

As she did so, she caught sight of the tissue-wrapped valentine which she had kept in her hand when she came down from the attic.

She looked about her for a convenient receptacle for it, and just as Miss Payne's foot touched the door stone, she succeeded in inserting it in her own square work-bag, hanging near.

"Good afternoon, 'Cretia! You are a stranger. Come right in and set by the fire. What a pretty day we've had, but ain't it sloppy?"

"Yes," 'Cretia assented. "It is dreadful sloppy, though it's been a nice day."

She went to the fire and sat down, replying briefly and absently to Mrs. Wills' cheerful talk.

And the latter said by-and-bye:

"You look beat out, 'Cretia. Ain't you well? You'd better take off your things and stay the evening, or over night. Do."

Her visitor roused herself.

"Oh, yes. I'm well—middlin'. But I was up most of the night. I've been over to Mrs. Gruer's. I suppose you didn't know she was taken yesterday, very sick and sudden?"

Mrs. Wills turned pale.

"Taken?" she asked, breathlessly. "How? When? I didn't know—"

"Taken down sick all at once—pretty near pnewmony, so the doctor said. And he's afraid of a fever, anyway, though he's doing his best to break it up. Lute Garvin—he does the chores and stays there nights, you know—came over after me, and I went right over and stayed till now. I'd have stayed to-night, too, but Harrett, she's all tired out and about sick herself, on account of the children. Measles, you know, and all at once, but they came out nice and they're doing well now, and I felt as if I'd got to get back. And that's what I came in for, to see if you wouldn't go over to Mrs. Gruer's and watch to-night; she's all soul alone, but Luther—or," she added, hastily, "if it wasn't so'st you could go, if you didn't know of somebody that could? And maybe get word to her. I would, myself, only it's so late, and I'm a good two miles from home," she explained.

"Why, I'll go, myself, of course, 'Cretia," Mrs. Wills hastened to say. "And I'm sure I'm much obliged to you for letting me know. Roger's doing the chores now, and I'll let him get his own supper on, for once, and I'll put my things on and go right over. You'd ought to have sent word to me before," said she, reproachfully, but flushing as she said it. "Did the doctor leave any word about the medicine or anything? And isn't there something I could carry over? The store is some ways off."

"Not a thing, Mrs. Wills, everything is there and handy. She even happened to have done a baking that day, and there's victuals a-plenty. And the directions the doctor wrote out on a slip of paper that lies beside the glasses. The drafts on her feet will want to be changed, and maybe, if she can stand it, there'd better be another mustard-plaster put over her chest. That's all. Oh, I forgot, he did say she must have all the nourishment she would take. Hot milk, or tea and toast, or gruel with cream, or anything like that. He wants to keep her strength up."

Ten minutes later, Mrs. Wills was walking swiftly across the crusted fields toward the brown cottage. There had been a little foot-path, well-trodden, always, between the two houses in the old days—for it chanced that neither of them had left, at her marriage, her childhood's home—and Mrs. Wills thought of it now with a sigh.

As she approached the house, she saw, through an open barn-door, Luther, lantern in hand, and his arm strung with milk pails, go-ing to do his "chores."

She let herself in noiselessly. The house was very still, but warm and inviting, even in the twilight.

She laid down her work-bag—her knitting would be company in the night-watches—and she had thrust into it, besides a clean apron or two, her glasses and an unopened box of mustard, lest the supply might run low when it was most needed. And she took off her shawl and hood, and hung them in the side entry, noting as she did, through the open door, the extreme neatness and the refined and cheerful homelikeness the vista of long, low rooms revealed.

"Lucinda was always just so handy! 'Twas born in her, a real god-mother gift, I used to tell her. And it looks as if she'd somehow took a good deal of quiet comfort here right along."

She still spoke of her neighbor in the past-tense, and when she entered her bed-room, the sight was not re-assuring. The sick woman was drowsing, a feverish spot on either cheek, while one thin hand, hot to the touch, lay on the coverlet, twitching nervously.

The bed-clothes were pulled to one side, and the pillow crumpled and aslant. Mrs. Wills straightened the blankets and deftly turned and smoothed the heated pillow, inserted a smaller one beneath it to rest the tired shoulders, and all without disturbing the sleeper. Then she stood looking at her a moment, while a great tear welled slowly from either kindly eye. She patted the quilt beside the restless hand, less uneasy now, and went softly out.

In the kitchen she became herself again.

"What next I wonder? Lights after fires, and these are all right. I believe 'Cretia trimmed 'em all to-day, they're so full and shiny." She lighted two or three, and set one, well-shaded, in the farther room. Stove and furniture shone in the lamp-light, and the tea-kettle was singing.

Stands filled with thrifty plants, well-tended and blooming, occupied three windows. Their leaves were green and glossy, and the air was almost heavy with their fragrance. The scents oppressed her vaguely, and a tall calla lifted its great snowy cone so ostentatiously that she was glad to look away from it. By this time Luther had come in, and she questioned him closely. Hope returned as she did so, for the doctor, it seemed, had spoken for the most part most encouragingly.

Supper was eaten, and Mrs. Wills was washing the dishes in the well-ordered pantry, when a sound came from the sick-room. She had looked in before, but had found her charge still sleeping. Now Mrs. Gruer had raised her head, and leaning on her elbow, looked confusedly around her.

But she sank back again, wearily, submitting to be tucked in warmly again, and receiving meekly both medicine and gruel from her nurse's hands.

She gave an earnestly curious look at last into Mrs. Will's face, smiling back trustfully as the other smiled at her. Then she lay down again and soon was sleeping quietly.

"She don't rattle a mite, and her cough ain't so bad," said Mrs. Wills, running back to where Luther sat, struggling with cube root.

"I do feel to be encouraged."

And all night long, while she sat watching, with Luther breathing heavily in the chamber above and her charge sleeping softly beside her, her courage waxed.

The east was rosy with the near, late dawn, when for the twentieth time she felt her patient's pulse, and touched her cheek, and listened to her breathing. Each time her heart had grown lighter, and now she said:

"She's going to get well! I never saw any-one come out of it better!"

She slipped away into the kitchen where the fire was already crackling.

Presently, when Mrs. Gruer had wakened, a tiny round table stood beside the bed, with a white cloth laid over it, and dishes for two persons upon it. There was besides, a plate of delicately browned toast, a tumbler of crimson jelly, a tiny block of riven, dripping honey comb, on a glass plate, and a dish of wheat, with a tiny flagon of cream. And the steaming tea-pot came in in Mrs. Wills' hand. Their eyes met and lingered in the look they gave each other.

"How do you feel? And will you let me bathe your face and hands and give you a cup of tea? You must be faint."

"I believe I am hungry," said the invalid, submitting to the application of the hot, wet towel. "That is refreshing! Your breakfast looks so tempting, and the tea smells so nice! How good you are, Frances! But," wistfully, as the other waited, "you're going to eat with me?"

"Well, I guess so," sitting down beside her. "You see I've got to get home by sun-up. Roger's so helpless! But I'll be right back, and stay all day. Now do eat. You must!"

"You're so good," the other said again. "I shall be up and dressed by-and-bye."

"Not to-day ! Perhaps, if you gain a lot, to-morrow. I want you to be careful," she went on, half bashfully, "and get on the faster. You know the sewing circle meets with me next week, and I've been wondering since I see you was coming out of it so well, if you couldn't come over, being well wrapped up, and stay over night with me ! I'd love to have you !"

"Why, of course I can," Mrs. Gruer replied, "and I thank you !"

The little meal was ended. It seemed almost like a sacrament, strengthening both heart and body. Mrs. Wills removed the table, arranged the invalid comfortably, donned her things, and came back to the bedroom, her workbag in her hand.

"I bought this for you forty years ago," she said, huskily. "And I wrote your name and mine on it. Will you take it now? I never saw anyone else," she went on, laughing tremulously, "that those verses would fit."

She laid the faded valentine on the bed, and her friend's hand clasped her own and, it together.

A FAST DAY SERMON.

Pastor Allan did not preach it, nor hear of it, though he rejoiced in the events which were its results. And it was not preached in the church at all, but in Mary West's kitchen, where there were only two people present, and those two were alternately preacher and hearer. An odd discourse, was it not, even for Fast Day? But then, it wasn't preached on Fast Day,—all of it.

It happened on this wise. Captain Simon Eastman, on an April morning, dropped in at his neighbor, John West's, to see what he had concluded to do about seed-potatoes. John had gone to town, but his sister Mary, who lived with him, was stepping briskly about her sunny kitchen, where spicy odors of the morning's baking mingled with the scents of the oleander and heliotrope and geraniums in the south windows. "John has gone to the store," she said, "but I expect him back right away now. It's been most two hours since he went, and if he didn't have to go to the corner, he'll be here soon. Sit down, Squire, and wait for him, if you aren't in a hurry. There's yesterday's *Journal* on the stand, and won't you try my caraways while you wait?" And she placed a blue china plate piled with crisp, sugary cookies before the caller.

"Thank you, Mary, I *will* stop a bit, and see if he don't come." And the Squire seated himself in the old-fashioned, calico-covered rocker by the window, and unbuttoned his overcoat, helping himself to the cookies, but not unfolding the paper beside them.

"These are first-rate jumbles," he said presently, "and good-looking pies these are, too. My mother can't beat either of 'em, I declare. But," he added, with a quizzical twinkle in his keen gray eyes, "seems to me it ain't quite seemly in you to be doing all that baking the day before Fast Day. Always thought you was right strict about such things. But times have changed, and maybe you've altered in your views," with another mirthful gleam in his eyes. "No blame to you if you have, I'm sure, I don't believe there's many of your church members but have."

The color began to burn in Miss Mary's cheeks, and her eyes had an ominous sparkle. She put the last pie away carefully in the pantry, and came back to the now empty oven to put a roast of veal therein.

"No, Squire Eastman, I hain't changed my views at all, and no more my customs. I keep Fast Day as faithful as I ever did. But you know John ain't of my way of thinking. Sundays he keeps like a Christian, if he don't belong to the church, as I wish he did; but, like you, he don't want to go without his victuals any day in the year. And he'll work to-morrow, if nothing happens, the same as he does to-day, and expect his meals the same, and so with his help. And though I'd rather have it different, still I can't help seeing what my duty is, both ways."

"And very good and accommodating of you, I'm sure," interpolated her listener.

"But," Miss West went on, while her eyes grew brighter, and the flush on her cheeks deepened to a livelier red, "I think, as I always did, that it's a pretty slimpsy kind of religion that can't or won't take one day in the year to take its bearings, and throw off ballast, as you'd say, being a sailor once. We're all poor creatures, perishing ourselves,

and using the things that perish in the using.
And we're that short-sighted, we mistake, a
thousand times, that that's passing away for
that that's going to last through all eternity,
and put the fleeting things first, and get to
loving 'em the best.   And we're all prone to
evil, and we get into evil ways of one kind
and another without realizing it.   It's Jude,
ain't it, that says, 'Keep yourselves in the love
of God;' but I think it's our duty to take ourselves in hand sometimes, and consider our
ways, and maybe get some of that humility
and contriteness that never fails of the Lord's
forgiveness and help and blessing."

The Squire had risen, and was pacing back
and forth in the sunny room, now and then
parting his lips to speak but refraining till she
paused.

"All that is true, Miss Mary, and I don't
doubt you live up to it. But I s'pose you know
there's lots of your folks that make that kind
of thing an excuse for the other things they
don't do, and don't mean to do, a kind of 'cloak
of covetousness.'   There's the Widow Emery,
that keeps boarders down on the plain, and
skimps every meal she sets out, they say,
being the only one handy there, and putting
money away every month, regularly.   She

keeps Fast Day, and her household,—*they* have to; and she believes in it. And our neighbor, Deacon French, he won't run his manufactory to-day, and his help must all lose it; for of course he takes it out of their pay, though he knows how terribly they need every cent they can get, with the hard times, and cut-downs and shut-downs this winter. And French is able to do differently, or I wouldn't blame him. And there's a dozen others will keep Fast Day, and maybe save a dollar by doing it, when they wouldn't think of giving a day or a dollar to help them that's suffering and needy. They leave most of that for us sinning outsiders to do. Oh! you know I don't mean you, Mary, so you needn't feel hurt. Now, there's poor Jim Carver, laid up with rheumatism half the time, with six puny children and a sick wife. And Carver's as good and true a Christian as ever lived in Clayton, and so is she. I declare, I can't believe Christians have a right to sit down and fast and pray even *one day*, when they should be using time and money to do something for Jim, and the like of him. John, you know, who ought to have known Christ better than Jude, humanly speaking, says, 'He that loveth not his brother whom he hath seen, how can he love God whom he hath not seen?' 'And whoso hath this world's good and seeth his brother's need,' and doesn't have compassion,— you know John asks again, how can God's love be in such a one? And, 'If God so loved us, we ought also to love one another.' I've never said much about it, Mary, but for a good while I've called Him Master, and tried to follow him. And I think he accepts me and my love, though I don't feel to profess anything yet. And I can't think I could serve and honor him better than by going round bit and helping poor folks, or sick folks, or anybody that's in any trouble, a little like he did! But there's John, and I think I'll go out to the barn and talk with him while he unharnesses. I'm in something of a hurry."

And the Squire took his hat and was gone, leaving his auditor in wondering silence. She sat still for some time, oblivious, for once, to the fact that the fire was low, and the meat needed basting, and, as she would have phrased it, "the forenoon was going." And she said only, as at length she went about her tasks again :—

"Well, I do wish he'd stayed long enough for me to ask something more about the Carvers. I hain't been in there for a few days, and don't really know whether either of them is able to stand company, or anything." With which apparently irrelevant remark she addressed herself to her tasks with renewed diligence.

It was late in the afternoon, when coming home from a round of calls, every one of which had compassed an errand, and nearly every one been on some brother or sister in the church, that Miss West found herself face to face again with her caller of the morning.

"I've been looking for you, Squire Eastman. I wanted to see you first thing, but you'd gone. You see," she went on, "I—that is, we—thought we couldn't do better than take to-morrow, or a part of it to help the Carver family. (Perhaps you don't know, but the church *has* helped them regular, since last November. But that's neither here nor there.) Mr. Allan thinks it an excellent idea, and even offered to change the meeting-hour, if 'twould do any good. But we thought, all taking hold so, there'd be time enough after service. I should have waited to get your opinion about it, but there was no time to lose. But I was pretty sure you'd approve of it. You know there's those front rooms Jim's been trying so long to finish and get into. Those rooms would be ever so much more comfortable now that it's growing warmer and the spring rains are coming on. Well, the men are going over first, with their tools and such, to put things in shape (we're going to get the family off for the day) ; and then we women are going to take hold and fix up the rooms as nice as ever we can. We shall do some papering,—the rooms are all plastered,—and quite a lot of people have promised furniture, or bedding, or dishes, for they're out of everything, most. And then everybody's going to bring something, so to stock up the pantry, you know. 'Twill be a good thing for the family, don't you think so?"

"Splendid!" exclaimed the Squire. "Why, whatever made you think of it, Mary? 'Twill be a great lift for 'em, sick and discouraged as they are. And if everybody takes hold, it can't help getting done up in good shape. Oh! I'll be on hand. Nobody could have planned it any better. I'll be in maybe, this evening ; and anyway, if you want anything I've got or can do, just let me know."

April never brought a lovelier day than the holy-day that followed, consecrated by formal proclamation and by consenting hearts—by the former to penitence and prayer and praise, by the latter to loving deeds of earnest Christian helpfulness. The morning was quiet. The prayer-meeting, larger, and richer and fuller of blessing than usual, with its warmer prayers, earnest confession, and deepened faith and feeling. But the afternoon was busy indeed. Too busy, one or two thought, for Fast Day, but only one or two. And the Carvers made amends, when it was discovered to them in all the comeliness and comfort of the rejuvenated home, by turning it into Thanksgiving Day, instead.

"Mary," said Squire Eastman, as the day was waning, and the workers were separating in the fast-gathering dusk, "I don't want you to think I don't appreciate all this the folks have done here. They've done well, and they mean right, all of 'em, I don't doubt. And we've all faults enough of our own. And I didn't think, really, they would turn out and work like this. I'm afraid I wronged 'em in my heart, judging them so."

But she answered, "I don't mind your wronging us a little so much. But I can't help thinking, though, that you *are* wronging the Lord. If you're his, doing all these things for him and out of love to him, don't you think folks ought to know it? Wouldn't it come nearer to honoring him, so? And if you belong to him, don't you want to belong to his church, and be known for one of his household ?"

And she was the only one, save perhaps Mr. Allan, who was not surprised when, a few weeks later, Squire Eastman made confession of his faith by baptism, and was received into the fellowship of the Clayton church.

SIMON NEAL'S CHARITY.

He was riding leisurely homeward one June afternoon, when the idea first came to him. He had his Thursday's mail in his pocket, and as he slackened his rein for the ascent of one of the steep, rocky hills between Stanford Village and Hillside Farm, he drew out his *Journal*. He had read little when, as he unfolded the sheet, he chanced upon a notice to the effect that the Fresh Air Association was about to begin its summer's work; that funds were already in hand and other contributions would be gratefully received; and that any persons willing to receive one or more of the needy city children into their homes for a short time, might address the manager of the association at 1850 Blank street. He read the item twice, then folded the paper and put it away. And for the remaining three miles before they reached the Farm, Sol, the hand-

some, intelligent bay, felt that his master was
pre-occupied. But this pre-occupation shall
give us opportunity to observe more closely
this man with the bronzed cheek and the
kindly smile, and to read, as story-tellers may,
his history and his environment. His hair is
white, though he is but fifty; the eyes are
grey, wistful and gentle. A kindly smile
plays sometimes about the set lips. A look
as of loneliness is in the steady eyes; and he
has an air of self-mastery that distinguishes
him from most men.

Twenty years ago, he, then not yet thirty,
had brought to the pleasant farm which was
his inheritance, his young wife, Hannah. A
gentle woman, with a sweet voice, a willing
hand, a true and trustful heart. Life had
gone well with them for a few years, and its
best gifts had been showered upon them.
Then, without a warning, sickness came,—
diphtheria, malignant, fatal,—and in three
short weeks Simon Neal sat in his desolate
house, bereft of wife and children. He had
neither brother nor sister to soothe his maddening anguish, or help lift the burden of his
lonely sorrow. How he lived for months
afterward he neither knew nor cared, nor
could he afterward bear to remember. The

6

faces of neighbors irritated him. Their well-meant consolations seemed maddening mock-eries. His work, his farm, his business, went whither they would.

But at length light dawned on this chaos. A friend of his boyhood, Julian Kirle, came to Stanford to preach in the little church. And the minister, finding among the souls he fain would shepherd, this school-mate, Simon Neal, so sorrowfully changed, spared neither sympathy, effort, entreaty, prayer, nor anything that Christian brotherliness could devise, to win the sorrowing man to the light that could alone illuminate his dark way,—"the Light that lighteth every man that cometh into the world." And at last the pastor's efforts availed. Slowly, hesitatingly, Simon Neal opened the doors of his desolated life,—opened them Heavenward that God's love might come in,—opened them earthward and outward that living help might go to those in any need. And so at last peace came.

He still lived alone. Near kindred he had none. A cousin, Martha Spear, whose husband's farm adjoined the Neal homestead, kept the few rooms he used in order, and washed and churned and mended for him. She cooked his simple food, such as he did not himself prepare, for he was "handy as a woman and as neat as wax, himself," the neighbors said.

But by this time Sol has climbed the last hill, has entered the wide-open gate, and paused at the door. And as the master of the house roused himself from his reverie and sprang out he ejaculated, "I'll do it."

And Sol pricked up his long ears, turned his great brown eyes to look, and whinnied a satisfied assent.

The horse was groomed and stalled and fed. Barn and shed and stable were locked after the cows had come up the lane and been milked. The tea-kettle he had put on over a freshly kindled fire was singing cheerily when at last he was ready for his solitary supper. Solitary, yet neither untidy nor uninviting. His deft and accustomed hands soon made ready the meal, and the tired man ate and drank. It was a quaint and cheerful room, neither kitchen nor parlor nor dining-room, but serving for all three, a "living-room."

The bright yellow floor shone with varnish and cleanliness. On the painted walls hung various relics of by-gone days. A brass-framed mirror hung over the low mantel, and gay everlastings stood in tall vases below it. An old-fashioned, many-shelved dresser revealed stores of dainty and curious china, and other pieces, fragile and quaint were on the crimson covered tea-table. Opposite the dresser was a tall secretary, its deep shelves overrunning with books new and old. A stand beside it held yet other books, and piles of papers and magazines. A slender vase, with June roses in it—had Martha Spear placed it there, or the master's hand?— stood there, and the sweet, subtle odor mingled with the scents of summer-time that stole through the half-open window.

Simon Neal finished his supper and put away the remnants thereof. He fed the great yellow cat that followed him about, and—laugh not, O more masculine, less "handy" reader—he washed and wiped and put away his few dishes and the strainer and milk-pails. Then he seated himself at his desk in the secretary, and wrote a letter. It was addressed to 1850 Blank street, and was such a letter as the manager of the charity whose office was at that number did not often receive. In the letter he offered to receive into his home for the month of July some needy child, a little boy it must be, and he told also, as in honor bound, something of his circumstances, promising good food and care, and referring to the village clergyman. He enclosed, also, a check large enough to send 'two or three poor waifs many miles into the country. He was on his way to town with it next day when it occurred to him that he ought to consult his good cousin Martha. So he stopped there.

"Martha," said he, "I don't know as I ought to have done it without asking you, but the letter isn't mailed yet—I've written to tell 'em I'd take one of their starving gamins a few weeks, fresh air charity, you know, I could take care of some youngster as well as not. Should rather like it if he's the right kind."

"Take a boy?" echoed Mrs. Spear, thinking it would be much more to the purpose if he would take a woman and a wife. "Oh! I understand now. A visitor, you mean. Well, I don't know, Simon, it might be a good thing for you, and then again it mightn't. But it wouldn't make any odds to me, 'twon't be any more work hardly."

And Simon mailed his letter. The manager at 1850 read it with some surprise and more than once. Then she read it aloud to two or three lady members of the board who chanced to be in the office at the time.

"Do you know of any child that ought to go?" she asked. "You see he wants one boy, a month. A week apiece for four boys would do more good."

"No," said Mrs. Harrington, one of the most active of the advisory committee, "I know of a child to whom and to whose mother it will be a providence. Mrs. Hart, on Pleasant street; she is ill; must go to the hospital for a while for treatment. She has only this one, a boy of six, and her means are small. They're not at all common poor people, and I'm sure this Mr. Neal, or whoever he is, would like Bennie. I will see the mother myself to-night."

So Mary Hart, a widow who supported herself and her child by middle class dressmaking found her burden of anxiety a little lightened by our friend's offer. She had hardly known which way to turn, as her health gave way, and she felt every day taking something from her little savings, and from her strength. She could go to the hospital—that had been arranged—and there seemed a hopeful certainty that a few weeks' sojourn there would restore in great measure her accustomed health. But in the meantime, what would become of Bennie, her earthly all? This question had haunted her by day and by night. A thousand plans had presented themselves, to be rejected.

"Where will Bennie go while mother goes to the hospital to be made well?" she asked him, at last, one day, in despair.

The child's eyes deepened and then brightened.

"I'll go off into the green country," he said, "where the little birds and the chickens and the lammies are." And he clapped his hands.

And now, behold! that was where he *was* going. Mrs. Harrington had brought the letter and left it with her, and the mother read it many times between the lines and carefully. Something about it reassured her. It could not seem otherwise than the one thing, and a safe, good thing for Bennie to do.

Yet it was with a very heavy heart, burdened more for him than for herself that she bade him good-bye, and went to bear the pain that awaited her.

Mr. Neal was waiting his little guest at Stanford Station. It was five o'clock in the afternoon, and the countryside was very fair to look upon as they rode along. Mr. Neal scanned the little face with its great brown eyes, intently. He saw with satisfaction the look of pleasure deepen and grow more radiant as vista after vista of green fields and scattered farms, and tiny villages, and sparkling, emerald-fringed lakes and azure hills opened before them as they rode onward. And he noticed, too, the exquisite neatness that marked the child, his evident refinement and the stamp of worthy lineage he bore.

"I guess he'll do! And I *think* he'll like pretty well, too," he said to himself. And so it proved. Unalloyed joy, but for the absence of his mother, filled the long summer days for Bennie Hart. The old-fashioned farm house, with its quaint belongings, was beautiful to him. The fields about were full of "unexplored remainders" in the shape of flower and tree and berry, bird and grasshopper, and butterfly. The half-neglected garden and the shady orchard were a dream of delight. While barn and shed and work-shop never lost their fascinations. He was a frank and truthful little fellow, with only the natural roguishness of childhood, and a boy's inquisitiveness. And there was a certain happy winsomeness about him that made him liked at once.

They were happy weeks fo Mr. Neal too. It was pleasant to see that little china bowl and plate opposite his own place, and to make ready 'the child's bread and milk before he drank his own coffee in the sunny, cheerful mornings. And it was right good to see that bright face *tete-a-tete*, where he had been solitary so long. This child-guest too, failed so far of filling the place of his own loved ones, that it was hardly a painful reminder of his losses.

"I declare," said Mrs. Spoor, one day, to her husband, as she returned from her cousins, "I have not seen Simon in such good courage for a long time. That child perks him right up. Seems if 'twas just what he wanted."

Mary Hart wrote frequent letters to her boy, letters which his host must read to their pleased recipient. And he volunteered to be amanuensis to Bennie, for he knew the mother's heart must crave news of her darling. And he sometimes enclosed a few lines on his own behalf to assure her of her boy's well-being. And indeed the child throve wonderfully at Hillside Farm. A more boyish beauty began to take the place of the child's delicate winsomeness. And when it seemed probable that Mrs. Hart would not be able to leave the hospital so soon as she had hoped, Bennie's friend was only too glad to write and offer to keep the child through August also, or even longer.

So it was that in the golden sunset of a September day a slender dark-clad woman walked hesitatingly up the yard after the East Stanford stage had rumbled by, and knocked at Simon Neal's door. He sat at his tea table, though the meal was done, and Bennie had slipped from his stool and was deep in some illustrated books on the table in the farther corner of the room.

"Excuse me, sir, but does Mr. Simon Neal live in the neighborhood?"

He had not time to answer, for Bennie had caught his mother's voice and was in her arms almost before the question had passed her lips. But when she had satisfied her longing eyes with the sight of the boy's now round and rosy face, his sturdier limbs, and his own brown, answering eyes, Mr. Neal came forward to beg that she would sit and rest and, before she could refuse, had poured for her a cup of tea, hot, fragrant, stimulating, with real cream, moreover. Faint from her journey and its excitements, she could but partake, wondering much at the house and its owner, yet wondering not at all that Bennie loved him and that she had instinctively trusted his letter. But she soon recollected herself, the time, the place, the host.

"A bit of unlooked for good future in the payment of an old debt, made it possible for me to do what the doctor advised so strongly, take a trip into the country. So of course as soon as I could travel, I came to find Bennie," she explained. "And I never can tell you how much I thank you for all your great kindness to him."

"Not at all, madam; I am the debtor for the boy's companionship. Right good comrades, we are, eh, Bennie? But, Madam, you must not go back to the hotel; here is my cousin, Mrs. Spear; her summer boarders went last week, and she has plenty of room, and would make you welcome." So, with Bennie to pilot her, Mrs. Hart went back to the house she had passed a little before, and Mrs. Spear, as her cousin had promised, gave her hospitable welcome. Mrs. Hart stayed there a month, first as boarder, then half-guest, half-seamstress, putting in repair her hostess' simple wardrobe, while Bennie vibrated between the farms. Then, loath to leave Stanford, with its pure air, its lovely hills, its honest friends, its atmosphere of kindliness, she rented rooms in the town, and put out her sign, "Dressmaking." And she was soon earning enough to make her comfortable, contented, hopeful.

It was hard for Mr. Neal to part from Bennie.

"Didn't know how much I *should* miss the little chap," he mused over his solitary breakfast, the day after Bennie's departure. But he had the boy out for little visits every now and then,—a night, or a day, or over Sunday, whenever he could get his mother to spare him. And always, when the farmer went to town, he carried something for Bennie, Tallman sweets, Nodheads, or Blue Pearmains; winter pears, or nuts, or pop-corn; yellow crook-necked squashes, some of the butter and cheese Bennie like so much.

"Really, Mr. Neal," said Mrs. Hart one day, as he came in, burdered as usual, "I think you are 'most too kind to Bennie."

"Oh, them apples came off Bennie's tree, you know."

"But the butter, and the vegetables, and the potatoes."

"Well, Bennie helped hoe, didn't you, lad? And we took care of the things together, didn't we?"

"But at this rate," said the mother laughingly, "he would have an interest in half the farm!"

"It rather looks," said Mrs. Spear, one day, "as though Hillside might some time have a mistress as well as a master. And I'm sure I hope so. But, then, you never can tell. If only the gossips don't spoil it all!"

The gossip's tongues *were* busy—so busy that Mr. Neal began to go less frequently, and Mrs. Hart to invent excuses for denying

Bennie some of his frequent visits to the farm. But the boy had a severe illness in April, and nothing could keep his good friend away. And when the child was convalescent, of course Mr. Neal must come often to see him and to take him to ride. And one May day, when Stanford and Hillside were every day taking on their old, familiar summer beauty he came in, the boy being outside with his playmates.

"Nearly as well as ever, he is now," said his mother, "and gaining every day."

"Yes, he's picked up a good deal, I can see. Now if he only could come out to the farm for the summer, 'twould just set him up again."

"He don't seem to want to go away from his mother much yet," said Mrs. Hart, a little nervously.

"No," said Simon Neal, "he don't want to go without his mother. And I don't want him to. Can't you come Mary—to stay?" And Mary went.

FREE AND EQUAL.

The great barn doors were wide open, one east and one west, and the fragrant June wind drew in and out. The sun, nearing the horizon, shone in the west door on the littered floor and yawning mows. A row of patient cows, the sweet breath of the shady pastures in their nostrils, stood in the "tie-up," waiting the milker, who, milking stool in one hand, and milk pail in the other, advanced leisurely to his task. The slender, milky stream, flowing under his hand, beat a musical tattoo in the bottom of his tin pail for a minute or two, and as the pail filled up, the sound grew softer.

In the interval, the man became aware that someone was speaking, or reading, or declaiming, close by. Some sentences, enunciated with deliberate distinctness, reached his ears :—

"We hold these truths to be self-evident: that all men are created equal; that they are endowed by their Creator with certain unalienable rights ; that among these are life, liberty, and the pursuit of happiness."

Here the reader, or speaker, stopped.

"Freem ! Freem ! Can you hear that ?"

"Land alive, yes !"

"Every word, *plain*, you *sure*?"

"Every word an' letter."

"All right ! You know I've got to read the Declaration of Independence at the exhibition the night before the Fourth, and I thought I'd come out here and practice," and the boy returned to his retreat, in a high, far corner of the almost empty haymow, and to his oratorical practice, well content.

"Thought likely 'twas Roy, up to something or other," murmured the man. The pail was full, and a little snowy stream tinkled again in the bottom of another. It had died away into a softer flow, when Roy, beginning anew, pronounced again the words his one listener had caught before. They arrested his attention, and called into definite shape certain thoughts vaguely dawning within him. Some liberty-loving revolutionary spirit in the words took hold of him as there was need it should. Freem Burt had never declared his independence yet, though he was past twenty-two. Freem Burt, they called him, and he and they wrote it "Freeman," on the rare occasions when it was written anywhere. But he knew, if no one else did, that once it had been something else. "Free and Equal Burt" was the unusual name his half-drunken father had given the baby boy, long ago. The young man felt dimly its ridiculousness and its incongruity. And he felt, in a dumb, half-conscious fashion, its pathos. Little of boyhood's freedom, or manhood's liberty and equality, he had known. He had been bound out when a boy to a certain Barzilla Sparks. He had had, on the farm, food, shelter, clothing,—*work*: of the first three, a comfortable sufficiency; of the latter, an *un*comfortable abundance, and all of the coarsest kind. But it had been home to him, or all the home he had ever known. And even after his twenty-first birthday had come and gone, and his twenty-second, he had stayed on. Squire Sparks was glad enough to have him, though he turned deaf ears to the hints the man dropped regarding the wages that ought now to be his.

"You have what you need, don't ye, Freem?" he would say. "You don't go hungry ever, nor suffer for nothing, do ye? 'A man's wages' that you're harping about,—a man's wages, is mighty uncertain. If you git your keep, you've got it about all. That's all I git;" and the master of the farm would go off to his desk in the "sittin'-room," to reckon the interest due on certain mortgages, or consider the disposal of the quarter's gains from farm and store and mill. And the next time he went to town, he would bring home a new pair of stout shoes, or a pair of coarse pants, or a straw hat, or, if it were winter, a gay "comforter," for the man.

If he had known what was working in Freem's mind, he would doubtless have dealt more liberally with him. The "man's wages" Freem coveted, as manhood's due, the Squire would have paid, and more than that, rather than part with him. But Freem's thoughts were his own, and he shared them with no one. And it was as well that he should not be made content, even for a time, at the Sparks' homestead. Freem felt this, dimly, himself. From the door of the "tie-up" he could see the spreading boughs of the trees in the great orchard. He knew how much of the small, puckery fruit went into the cider-mill; he knew his own work in connection therewith,— work that he despised and dreaded, though it had its pleasures.

But Freem had signed Roy's temperance pledge a little while ago, and he meant to keep it. This much of manliness he wanted to hold to. Perhaps, by-and-by, it would lead to something more. But he could not keep that pledge where he was, he knew well. And he had begun to feel, too, even before he signed it, that it was going to be harder for him to hold to clean, sober, manly habits, every year he lived there. Yet the place was dear to him; all the best years of his poor life had been spent there. He had never known anything like comfort, or the certainty of hardly the next poor meal, or a clean, warm bed, before. And, though he hardly owned it to himself, I think he rather distrusted his power of making his way among men in the world, even in a poor, toilsome fashion. Of tramp-life he had an instinctive abhorrence and dread. He had no trade, and "dull times" were so sure to recur! If he had been certain of the poorest living, he would have gone forth long ago.

The closing sentence of the Declaration of '76, uttered and reiterated with varying inflections, and with all the sonorous emphasis Roy's boyish voice could give them, sounded in his ears as he finished milking. Freem went and stood in the door that opened toward the sunset. He was thinking hard,—so intently that he did not notice the hushed, cool world, so green and beautiful, nor the crimsoned skies, though he had always had a dumb delight in them and the twilight. Across the way was a little white house, where one of the Squire's employees lived,—John Mayne by name. There was a little garden at the side, and a tiny flower-bed in front. And John Mayne's wife was singing softly an old hymn, to the child going to sleep in her arms.

What might it be to have a home of one's own,—such a home as that! How hard and steadily a man could work, and take comfort in it, if it were for others, his own! Would the years ever lead *him* to such depths of joy as this? He hardly framed the question; it was a dumb yearning, rather than a wonder, in his heart.

But something whispered in him :—"Homes are for *men*, not for cowards!"

"I ain't a coward, an' I *won't* be!" said Freem Burt, resolutely, answering his own accusing thought. And with that he straightened up, took his brimming milk-pails, and went along the narrow little path through the grassy yard to the house. And that very night he told Barzilla Sparks, busy with his never-ending calculations at the old secretary, that he was about to look for work elsewhere.

To say that Squire Sparks was astonished, would be to state the fact very mildly. He regarded Freem as much a fixture as the beams in the old barn. So much astonished was he, he had at first no words at all. Then, recovering himself, and of course setting himself to the task of winning back his trusty help, he hardly knew whether to be indignant or facetious, and so was both alternately, at Freem's expense. But Freem was not to be moved. Slowly as he had come to his resolution of independence and its declaration, once made, every hour only confirmed him in it.

"Who is the knave," growled the Squire, "who has had the *despisable* meanness to come sneakin' 'round hirin' my man right out from under my nose?"

"'Tain't any one," returned Freem.

"Why, where ye goin'? Don't ye know what you're goin' to do?"

"I'm goin' to work and earn my own livin' —a man's honest, independent livin'," answered Freem, with some fire in his gray eyes. "I don't know where, yet, nor what."

Then was the Squire once more astonished. The idea that his man was leaving him for any other reason than the inducement of a good situation with some of the farmers around, or perhaps some simple assured employment in the village, had not occurred to him. But the facts re-assured him somewhat. Freem might look around a little, or even hire out somewhere through haying, but he would be glad to come back soon. A temporary absence, even at this busy season, might perhaps be put up with, for the sake of what might be later. He concluded it was best to play the part of friend and patron, and even conceal his ire.

"Well, Freem," he said, at last, "I hope ye'll prosper, I'm sure. An' don't be in a hurry about takin' your things away. Stay with us a few days while you're looking fer another job; you're welcome to. An' Mis' Sparks most likely'll have somethin' fer ye,— some socks or mittens, or a shirt or two, mebbe. An' come back an' see us when you get out of work, or have a chance."

Freem thanked him, and went out, thankful for a chance to stay a few days, till he should find his work, if it were near by, yet determined none the less to find it soon.

Nevertheless, the search proved not an easy one, nor soon successful. He started out with good courage, but every day lost a little of his hopefulness, as every place seemed closed to him. Where was the chance for him to be honest and independent, a man among men? Every avenue to manhood, as he understood it, seemed closed and barred to him. It was close upon haying time, and the farmers seemed all to have hired their hands for the season. Many of them knew him to be "good help," and would have been glad to hire him, had he appeared a little earlier. The Squire, meanwhile, was complacent and friendly. Things were turning out even better than he had hoped. Freem could not prosecute this hopeless search much longer; he would be glad to turn to with the rest next week in the haying field. And Freem was both discouraged and perplexed. He would have been even more despondent, but for John Mayne. This man was proving himself a friend in need and in deed. The little white house opened its doors to him of an evening or on Sunday, and Sunday was a pleasant day there. They made it holy-day and holiday, in homely country fashion. And every glimpse of this simple Christian home-life made Freem long for manhood's vantage, to win manhood's guerdons.

He had another friend, too, Roy Allen, the child of Squire Sparks' only sister, now in

California with her husband. Roy sympathized right heartily with Freem's efforts, and aided and abetted as far as lay in his power. His influence, though, seemed very little, and his help, also, for a time.

But it was through Roy, at last, that Freem's "chance" came. Roy had a friend, Hugh Clyde, of his own age, to whom, of course, he confided Freem's story. Hugh's father, Colonel Clyde, was the owner of a foundry in the town. And it transpired that there was need of another man, to do certain heavy work, for which no apprenticeship was necessary; and, hearing of Freem, and his struggle for independence, Colonel Clyde resolved to give him the place. Now, a foundry, of all workshops, was to Freem most fascinating. It had a stronger attraction than field or orchard, and the hot breath from the forge was sweeter to him than the wind from June meadows. The hammering, the forging, the riveting, and all the mysterious processes the metal went through, were to him full of charms. He longed, oh, how much! to be master of them all. And, lo, here was a chance to begin! It was on the Fourth that the good news came. John Mayne would take him for a boarder, and that very night Freem moved his belongings across the road.

And at twilight, as he stood in the door of the little cottage, and looked out into the free, wide world, so full of opportunities, it seemed as if indeed God's hand had set before him an open door.

A CHRISTMAS MESSAGE.

The evening express was late that night. There had been a broken wheel at starting, and then, when fairly under way, the train had been switched off at Waybury to let the night freight pass.

"The last switch, they say, between this and Waterton, and the freight train is due here in three-quarters of an hour. So, of course, it's our wait," said a gentleman who had been out to reconnoitre. "But we shall soon be under way again, and they'll put on steam enough to make up for this."

The passengers had begun to grow uneasy, there had been so long a delay already, and they knew that there was no station, not even a junction, at Waybury, in whose neighborhood they must be.

But this reassuring word quieted their apprehensions, and they settled themselves more con-

7

tentedly.　They were for the most part a cheerful company, or in a cheerful mood.　It was Christmas Eve, and "home for Christmas" seemed written in almost every face.

Among the few who were not homeward bound was the Rev. Arthur Avery, going to preach on the morrow—the day fell on the Sabbath—at Waterton.　He had been supplying there some weeks past, not as a candidate, they said, nor on trial, exactly; yet it was understood that "a call" would probably be accepted.　And the church, on the other hand, though it waxed critical over gesture, expression, manner, doubtless expressed itself through the senior deacon, who "didn't know as they could do better."

Meanwhile, Mr. Avery came up each Saturday night from Kingsford, the college town where he had been born and bred, where his parents still lived, where, for a year or two, pending a settlement, he had been serving in place of an absent professor, now returned, whither also, he had lately brought his young wife.

There was a sprinkling of scholarly men in the congregation at Waterton, as Mr. Avery was perhaps too well aware.　Judge Pitman, Doctor Andrews, Squire Holt, Lawyer Simmons, Mr. Burton, who edited "The Waterton News," and one or two others. And the prudential board had its share, the young minister knew. So he had not only been bringing his best sermons, from week to week, but exerting himself to prepare even better ones than the ministerial portfolio yet contained. It was this that began the trouble to-night. He did not use full notes or manuscript sermons, and the morrow's message was now maturing in his mind. The train of his discourse had suffered as many hindrances as the train that was bearing him on to preach it. Of course all the historical facts, and recondite allusions, and pertinent quotations he meant to introduce, he had carefully verified in his study. But the sequence of his topics was not quite clear, and the peroration refused to take shape at all. The talk and laughter around him irked and disturbed him.

"How long have we to wait, do you know?" he asked of his neighbor in front.

"Oh, a matter of an hour or an hour and a half, I should judge. I believe there are two freights to come down between this and midnight, and we're so late now we shall have to get clear of both of them."

The air in the car was hot and close; from a window opposite, open a trifle, came a breath of wind deliciously cool, and through the shadows outside he caught the gleam of a star.

"An hour yet and probably longer." Mr. Avery's head was aching, and he was tired. A brisk walk, he reflected, would quicken the vital currents of both body and mind. So a moment later he was pacing up and down the trodden snow between the tracks. The engine was panting beside him, and brakemen and switch-tender went to and fro, answering the enquiries of the others who, like himself, had sought the air. It was better than the stifling car, certainly. His head felt better already. But he could not think to advantage in the bustle, small as it was.

A little, beaten foot-path led up through the snow that clothed the fields, and betrayed the direction of the switch-tender's home. And in the near distance the minister saw the twinkle of scattered lights, put out one by one as the evening waned.

An hour yet!—and Mr. Avery climbed the gentle slope lifting his eyes to the stars, and baring his head for a moment with the involuntary feeling that he had stepped into a church—the night was so still, so serene, so solemn, the snow so pure, the starry canopy above him so vast yet so near. It seemed to him somehow like the first Christmas, when the world waited in such unconscious readiness and want for Christ's coming—such a great, mute expectancy was in earth and skies. So musing, he went on, till the whistle of an approaching train sounded below.

"Time enough yet," he thought, "for another train comes down by-and-by."

Turning leisurely, he retraced his steps—he had gone some distance through the fields—still without haste, for that application was taking point and polish very rapidly now. But he had not gone half-way down the hill when another whistle smote his ear.

The first freight had already passed; this must be the second, and two minutes later, this also, groaned by. Immediately the waiting train, all ready, evidently, for a new start, shifted to the other track, took breath in great, fiery gasps, and sped on its way.

The minister, meanwhile, had put on speed also, and reached the track as the train vanished round the nearest curve.

"Got left, didn't ye?" asked the switch-tender. "Well, now, that's too bad. They started up quite sudden at last; they always do. But if you aint going further'n Waterton, there's a special runs up there about daylight to-morrow morning—switches off here, too."

"That's just where I am going, if I have to walk."

"Oh, you're all right. If you'll only be on hand about day-break, or a little afore, I'll put you on as slick as can be. An' them specials go like the wind, you know—you'll be there in no time—but you must be here, and you needn't stay out doors all night, either."

"Oh, I shall do very well, I'm a good walker."

But the man shook his head.

"No need on't! Here's the Widder Kerle over here, her father's bad with asthma, he's had a terrible phthisicky spell; so she has to be up with him all times o' night. She'll take ye in, an' I'll go along with ye. 'Twon't trouble her any, she ain't that kind; wouldn't let a dumb critter lay out."

A few minutes later the man was knocking at the door of a wide house on the right of the widening path, and explaining his errand to the rather weary yet sweet-faced woman who answered the summons. She, too, insisted that our wayfarer was welcome, and, since he very positively declined supper and bed, left him in a comfortable, home-like sitting-room, where a great coal-stove gave out a delicious warmth, and a broad lounge, which she presently supplied with comfortables, promised rest.

"And you needn't worry about waking. I shall be up, I'm not going to bed anyway, I shall be up and down. And I always hear that train. And don't mind, please, if you hear us stirring. My brother is ill and suffering and my sister came home yesterday from the West with her little children—one very small. Good night, sir; I hope you will rest."

· She closed the door behind her, but another, partly open, led into the kitchen, whither, a little later, the minister, unable to sleep, saw his hostess go, followed by another woman, who was very like her only younger, smaller, slighter, and whose pale face, sad eyes, and mourning dress told of recent bereavement. A row of little stockings of graduated sizes betrayed their errand. They filled them together with presents, various and usually simple, from the long stockings dangling their brown legs in the corner beside the chimney to the wee pink sock by the stove. Before they were done a little wailing cry came from another room, and the mother answered it appearing presently with her baby in her arms, and sat watching her sister.

"Last year," she began, "their father helped me. I wasn't well, and he went out and got all the things. Such a good time as he made for them! This one wasn't here then—my poor, little fatherless child!" and the sobs came, and tears fell.

The other let her weep for a little, then she said:

"'A God of the fatherless' He is, and our brother."

"I know, I know! And I'm selfish to add a bit to your burdens—you, that know all about it, that have been through it all before me, long ago, and more. Lydia, how did you, how could you bear it so, and live on?"

The other did not answer for a little, and when she did, it was in words not her own—"'The Lord is my light and my salvation, whom shall I fear? The Lord is the strength of my life, of whom shall I be afraid?' 'I know that my Redeemer liveth.' 'Lo, I am with you always, even unto the end of the world.'"

She had taken the child now, and the flicker of the fire made a radiance about its head, and reflected the light of her own steadfast eyes. She looked as Mary might have looked with the child Jesus in her arms.

But she was talking now in an undertone: "I didn't know as I'd be able to get Rob's skates; and the magazine Jamie wanted so, I couldn't afford. The boys saved their pennies to get May that book, I knitted the purse, and the apron you brought is lovely. It takes such a little to please them. It isn't the worth of the gifts, nor even having the things, that they enjoy most I think. It's the Christmas cheer, I believe. I try to be happy with them, and it isn't hard, either. What a day Christmas is! The Day—for everyone. It takes in all blessings, doesn't it. And we feel it, like light or warmth, whether we realize all about it or not. I saw a picture once of Christ the Consoler, Christ our Comforter. I always think of it at Christmas time. Even when my sorrows were hardest to bear I was always glad of Christmas time. Lena, you must go straight to bed; I want you to let Rob get out the sleigh and take you to church in the morning. Elder Petus will be sure to have some good helpful Gospel word for Christmas Day. Seems as if every sermon was a special message of Christ."

The house grew still again, but Mr. Avery could not sleep. Not even after he had crept into the kitchen and slipped a shining silver coin into each stocking. What sort of a Christmas message would his elaborate discourse be to those in his congregation who were burdened with grief, or loneliness, or want, or temptation, or care? Was it really the good tidings of the living, loving, present Christ? Ah, what would the world be without Him? How truly he abode in this woman's heart, and in her home! And while he mused, there came a vision, infinitely precious, of how near God came when Jesus was born in Bethlehem; how, having entered into our human life—how deeply and really, and at what cost of suffering, only He can know—our Lord is still sharing it. How God sent, out of His love, His Son to declare Him and His love.

The clock in the corner chimed again, and a little later Mrs. Kerle appeared. But her visitor was all ready to go, thanking her heartily for her hospitality, but refusing to allow her to extend it further, even to include a cup of coffee, which she begged to make him. Half an hour later he had boarded the special, and was speeding towards Waterton, reaching the town just as the earliest sunbeams touched the spires, and ere the rose of dawn had faded from the Christmas skies.

It was noticed that Mr. Avery used fewer notes even than usual in the pulpit that day. Perhaps, his hearers thought, that was one reason why his message seemed so warm, so rich, so comforting. Ah! it could not fail to be—it was all about our Christ.

It would have done you good to hear the comments as the people went out.

"A real Gospel sermon," said Judge Pitman.

"It came right home," said the woman behind him, while her neighbor added, in a quavering voice—she was old and feeble:

"It done me a world of good."

Dr. Andrews pronounced it "a most excellent and timely discourse," while the editor declared in his turn, that—"it brought the real Christmas glow."

Mr. Avery did not hear all they said, but he did hear the call they unanimously extended at the very next church meeting, and he accepted it.

ONE EASTER DAY.

In the heart of a lovely bit of country, set in the shelter of clustering hills, Alan Brainerd's farm stretched east and west its fertile, well tilled acres. Silvery streams crossed its pastures, and here and there shone gem-like ponds—sapphire under the clear skies of May or November, emerald when June's greenness fringed their sloping banks, and changing to ruby and garnet when the October woods leaned over them, and dropped their burned-out leaves into the mirroring depths.

Close to old Blueridge itself grew the oaks and the birches of his woodlands, while down to the shores of Little River spread his well watered meadows and mellow wheat-fields. And severe indeed was the weather, when some of his numerous hands were not swinging the axes and driving the sleds in the former, or guiding the plow, the mower or the reaper in the latter.

The nucleus of it had been his father's and grandfather's homestead. Other lands adjoining, or so near that it was easy to secure the intervening acres, had become his by later inheritance. And by well-timed purchase, and in payment of long-standing debts, more had been added, until, looking from his piazza north, east or west, he could see only his own possessions. South of him ran the highway, and opposite, on the other side of the road, were farms with narrower frontage, stretching far back toward the lesser hills which faced Blueridge.

The house, in its outward appearance, at least, accorded well with its master. It was a grim, time-defying structure of stone. Its wide front and southern exposure, its terraced lawn and massive porch, its broad, little-used front door, and the quaint windows above the entrance that held the sunset light till they glowed like opals, all suggested gracious possibilities, but joyless actualities.

One thought, as one passed it for the first time, into what rich beauty the place might flower, if a glad household life were within it; and felt, even though a stranger, that its gray walls had not sheltered such an one for many a year.

And the man himself reminded you of something he was not, and seemed likely never to be. Tall, gaunt, muscular, with firmly set lips and keen, stern eyes, and a reserve neither audacity nor friendliness could penetrate, his neighbors would have found it easier to give him their sympathy and affection, even if unspoken, had he not so successfully guarded every avenue of approach.

Years before, so long ago that it was to his younger townsmen hardly more than a tradition, life had promised him very different things, and there had been in him, plainly seen, an answering potency that seemed likely to yield to his fellowmen rich revenues of helpfulness, a really noble fruitage of usefulness and influence. But long ere the vintage time, even in the ripening cluster, the wine had turned bitter and acid.

Old women talked of it sadly over their knitting or their teacups when they visited together, or were coaxed to tell it to their grandchildren in long summer afternoons or lonely evenings.

Mrs. Price, grandma to half the neighborhood, and young at eighty, sat one wild March day in the chimney-corner of the house opposite "the 'Squire's," as Alan Brainerd was always called when he had passed his youth. The smoke curled upward from his tall chimneys, plain even in the whirling snow, and, reminded thereby of the lonely master of the house, Barbara Price, a favorite granddaughter, began to beg for the story of his life, which no one could tell as grandma could, she said. "Tell about what changed him so," she added, "and makes him different from other people. Was it just his trouble?"

"'Just his trouble,' Barbara? Ah, you don't know what that was, I guess. Though I don't mean to say anyone has any right to let any sorrow the Lord sends spoil his life or make his heart bitter or cold. But I'll tell you about it.

"Alan was just twenty-two when he was married, and his wife was Mary Dunning. They had lived side and side all their lives, and set everything by each other. He brought her Mayflowers, and made her flower garden, for she hadn't any brothers; and he took her to school on his sled in winter-time, and filled up a corner of their attic for her, with nuts, and acorns, and traces of popcorn, in the fall. She never had a word for anybody else, and he never seemed to know there was any other girl round where she was.

"Well 's I said, they was married, and he took her home, and both their folks was well pleased. And they had two children, only a year or two apart, as bright and handsome as need be.

"Then, pretty soon,—they hadn't been married more than five or six years; I guess the boy, he was the oldest, wasn't quite four, and the girl maybe a year old,—trouble began to come, and it kept coming, and steady.

"First, his folks died, father and mother, and brother and sister. Then hers went, all but one sister, that she took home finally, to live with her. Then, as though 'twas coming nearer and nearer, they lost their little boy. That was a great stroke to 'em, I expect, but they bore up under it well.

"But it wasn't but a little while before she went, too, quite sudden, with quick consumption. And he's never been the same since, though he did have his little girl, for a while, and her sister to take care of her. Till by and by, diphthery came into the neighborhood— it was a dreadful time for all of us, I can tell you; and the little girl took it and died in three days, and then Nora Dunning, she took it, and come out of it, but never got her strength back, and died in three months in a decline. And that was all there was to go," the narrator added, soberly, wiping her eyes.

"Folks thought *he* would, and I guess he'd have been right willing, but the Brainerd constitution is beyond almost anything. He's had typhus fever since, and just pulled through. That was, let me see, fifteen, yes, twenty, years ago, more, for aught I know. He's been alone ever since. One of the solitary that aint set in families, here, I tell 'em. But I can't feel reconciled, not to see *him* reconciled, myself; and now I don't know as he ever will be. And still, I tell 'em, it may be only his way of taking it. We can't tell about such things."

"No, he hardly ever goes to a neighbor's or to see anyone. And, of course, bein' that's the case, hardly anyone goes there. But it isn't true what they say about his being stingy and snappish. I've lived by him fifty years, and I know better."

"He is very rich," said another listener.

"I suppose so. Yes, he must be, even for these days. But," with a flash of resentful indignation, "he isn't a miser! He just hasn't anything to do with his money. He can't use it, and hasn't any of his own kin to spend it on, and he don't see any other worth-while way to use it. I tell 'em Alan Brainerd got his death blow twenty-five years back, and has only half lived ever since. . I do sometimes think his spirit went when Mary's did, and just as truly.   Anyway, I haint seen anything that's looked like it since.   It ain't no more like him to settle down and scrimp and save, than nothing !   He just does it because there aint anything else for him to do.   He aint living, he's just staying, and has been.   I'm right glad he's going to Boston next week, if he is.   I think he ought to go off and stay quite a while, quite often."

Easter came betimes that year, early in April; and the month had already begun when Alan Brainerd set out on his journey. Up among the hills, and in Hilton itself, there were few signs of Spring.   Only the pussy-willows in the pastures, and the cawing crows in the woods, and perhaps an early bluebird, told that she was on her way.   The winds still swept across the fields and moaned among the pines, in whose shelter the arbutus still sheathed its buds.   Even the wind-flowers, frail and venturesome, had hardly looked out into the slowly softening air.   Meadow and brookside, and forest path, and pasture-knoll alike, were covered deeply with snow.

But here, whither he went, a little farther southward, and beside the sea, spring had al-

ready come.   Crocus-beds made bits of glowing color in the yards as he passed through the
suburbs, and the daffodils held up their sun-
filled cups in sheltered places.   In the florists'
windows were banks of purple violets, golden-
hearted pansies, white and crimson carnations,
and, outnumbering and outshining all the rest,
the stainless Easter lilies, for it was Passion
week.

Our friend saw the open church doors, and
read the announcements of the daily services,
but found no time to attend them.   Indeed,
the business he had planned to transact while
in the city might have filled a much longer
time than the few days he had planned to spend
there.   It kept him busy from morning till
night, and he found, when Saturday evening
came, that he should be obliged to remain some
days longer to complete it.   Besides, there were
on his list memoranda of calls to be made and
of purchases that could not be put off, while
he had meant to give a day or two to the
book-stores, and to take as long a time to go
about leisurely.   So he wrote to Burns, his
trusted man at Hilton, not to expect him until
that day week.

Easter Sunday was clear and bright.   The
sunshine came in at his window, and the

chimes played softly, gladly, tenderly, in the hour before church-time when he sat in his room, reading a little, thinking much, and re-membering, I am afraid, even on Easter Day, only, or chiefly, his griefs and loneliness.

But even the long-worn mail of his sorrows was not proof against all the sweet influences of the dear holy-day, whose hope sounded in the church bells, nodded in the flowers people carried in their hands, and shone in their faces. When the bells were ringing their last, swift peals, he joined the throng.

He had determined beforehand where he would go, partly out of a desire to see the building itself, for new Trinity was really new then, partly because of the fame of the preacher, and partly because of a genuine love for the ritual of the church. Of another com-munion himself, the "prayers of the ages" seemed to him to voice, as others rarely did, the heart's deep need. A prayer-book, worn with daily use, lay on his own study-table.

Following a beckoning hand as he entered the vestibule, he was led to a seat in the mid-dle of the church, beside a great pillar which threatened to shut quite from his view the face and form of the preacher. It did obscure it for some time, then, when the sermon was well begun, a movement of the other occupants of the pew caused our friend to change his position, softly, to lose no word of the eager message pouring torrent-like, from lips and heart of one who felt himself and proved himself a messenger of God; and he found himself facing the speaker, whose noble, benignant face, and glowing, steadfast, loving eyes interpreted as even his voice could not the words he uttered.

The years had brought to Alan Brainerd their own interpretations of his losses. He had, of late, especially, been ready to receive them, to see, if it had such, the nobler aspect of his grief. But such a message as this had never come before.

The sermon has carried, since that long ago Easter Day when it was first uttered, its great burden of hope and comfort to unnumbered hearts. It has been read in homes without number. There is hardly a discourse in all the matchless series that is lingered over more thoughtfully and thankfully. And upon this hearer the sentences fell like long-waited showers on thirsty fields that are withering in drought.

"It is the thought of an eternal God that really gives consistency to the fragmentary lives of men, the fragmentary history of the world.   A Christ that liveth, redeems and rescues into his eternity the broken, temporary lives and works of His disciples. * * * So long as there are men living and dying, so long above them and around them there shall be the Christ, the God-man, who liveth and was dead, and is alive forevermore.

"Let me show you the way into, the way through and the way out of this sorrow which you cannot escape.   Into it by perfect submission, through it with implicit obedience, out of it with purified passions and entire love. * *

"To-day we can see that duty is worth while.   Duty is the one thing on earth that is so vital that it can go through death and come to glory.   Duty is the one seed that has such life in it that it can lie as long as God wills in the mummy hand of death, and yet be ready at any moment to start into new growth in the new soil where He shall set it.   So let us all consecrate our Easter Day by resolutely taking up some new duty which we know we ought to do.   We bind ourselves so by a new chain to eternity, to the eternity of Him who for the joy that was set before Him endured the cross, despising the shame, and is set down at God's right hand. * * * * *

"In those moments when Christ is most real to me, when He lives in the centre of my desire and I am resting most heavily upon His help, in those moments I am surest that the dead are not lost, that those whom this Christ in whom I trust has taken, He is keeping. The more He lives to me the more they live. * * *

"I want to make you feel the force of the living Christ today. * * * If the city of our heart is holy with the presence of a living Christ, then our dear dead will come to us, and we shall know that they are not dead, but living, and bless Him who has been their Redeemer, and rejoice in the work they are doing in His perfect world, and pass on joyously to our own redemption, not fearing even the grave, since by its side stands He whom we know and love. * * * * * * *

"He is alive! Do you believe it? What are you dreary for, O mourner? What are you hesitating for, O worker? What are you fearing death for, O man? Oh, if we could only life up our heads and live with Him; live new lives, high lives, lives of hope and love and holiness, to which death should be nothing but the breaking away of the last cloud, and the letting of the life out to its completion!"

There was only the Recording Angel to register the vow, but, as the preacher ended, Alan Brainerd's heart made answer, silently, solemnly, fervently, "I will."

Then, like one of old, he "conferred not with flesh and blood," nor did he at first speak to any one of the message that had come to him that Easter Day, though the day had doubly fulfilled itself to him.

But Burns, when he met him some days afterward at Hilton station, ventured to say, discerning dimly something in his face that had not been there before:

"You're looking better, sir! Your trip has done you good, I guess."

"It has," said his master shaking hands heartily.

As was characteristic of the man, the change in him was made evident to his neighbors and townsmen slowly, and in unostentatious ways. Gradually they realized that if any one in the village needed a helping hand, "the Squire" was usually the first to offer it, and that no one was so swift to discern any want or trouble, or so skilful in alleviating it as he.

Little by little, the stone house relaxed its sternness. Roses grew again around the pillars and flower-beds around the terraces. The windows stood open all the June days through, and rustic chairs stood at hospitable angles on the piazzas. Flowers and fruit went from the gardens to the sick and poor, not to mention the more substantial gifts that orchard and granary furnished. The treasures of the library were again and again offered to ambitious and appreciative youth. The daughter of a far-away cousin, with her little crippled brother, found a home under the wide roof, and a life-long shelter under "the 'Squire's" generous care. Once or twice a season, too, the house was thrown open for a long delightful evening, and all the townsfolk were bidden in to greet its owner, share its good cheer, feast their eyes on its gathered treasures, and lose both prejudice and anxiety in its genial atmosphere.

The church was repaired, the minister's salary advanced, the academy endowed, a library established, and a variety of beneficent forces set in operation in the social life of the village—changes the older generation never ceased to wonder at, and the newer one accepted as a somewhat uncommon heritage; one to be prized and guarded, and which was enhanced, for a little, by the giver's presence among them.

But only for a little. Half a decade, already, has slipped away since; glad to go, he passed on—as has now gone the noble preacher to whom he owed so much and, all unknon, loved and reverenced so deeply—to the City that has in it no temple; "for the Lord God, the Almighty, and the Lamb are the temple thereof."

IN SAINT VALENTINE'S TONGUE.

The blackberry vines, whose ebon fruit there were so many little fingers to seize upon, were all invisible; and the February snows had draped the low, leafless sumachs, dwarfed by the drifts beneath, with clinging, frosty fleeces. The little, clumsily-framed building faced the north, so that no "ragged beggar" would seek the shelter of its rude porch. Otherwise, it was very like the schoolhouse that lived so long in Whittier's memory, and has been made imperishable in his tender lyric.

Stoutly built in the first place, time and the elements have touched it but lightly; and the "s'lectmen" of the town have felt themselves at liberty to let it alone, also. And so it stands with its "worn door-sill," its grimy, pencil-marked walls, and its rudely-shapen seats, whereon many a schoolboy has left his "carved initial"—perhaps the most enduring inscription

more than one of them has made—a model,
such as the Exposition, with all its relics, did
not hold, of the old-time district school.

Less than a score of years ago, at half-past
four on a mid-winter afternoon, more than a
score and a half of scholars poured out of it,
clutching their dinner-pails and seizing their
sleds, and carrying, too, with some care, cloth-
rimmed slates and calico-covered geographies,
for lessons were assigned to the older ones, at
least, on "the presumption of brains," and with
a thought of what might be done in the long
winter evenings.

Within were a half-dozen more, (it was a
large district and they had a popular teacher)
all save one of whom were scowling over a
mis-said lesson. That one, having replaced
the nails over one of the windows through
which the teacher had renewed the exhausted
air, hasped the cellar-door, and heaped up the
woodbox, stood by the stove in the chilling
room, waiting, yet not impatiently. The dingy
place was dear to him, dearer, maybe than to
any other. Shy, and awkward, even to un-
couthness, he stood twirling his faded cap and
scanning the algebra problems which the
teacher had just placed upon the blackboard,
and to some purpose, for before the dilatory

pupils had finished their tasks he had framed the last equation, pinning it down with a dogged mental repetition, absorbing, meanwhile, enough of the history questions that were being written beside them to put him a day in advance of his class, and leave to-morrow for its own recitations and the preparation which must immediately precede them. For the longest, darkest evening brought little leisure to him.

It was later than usual when teachers and scholars had at last turned from the door stone, and he might lock the heavy door, pocket the cumbrous key, and go his way. He remembered as he did so that "the Squire" had gone to the county seat to attend court that day, and would not be home till late at night, and that he had been charged to bring home the mail. There were many chores, too, to be done before supper time.

So he stepped off briskly, losing some of his awkwardness when he was by himself in the open air, with the glowing skies and snow-wrapped hills looking down upon him, and quickening into consciousness within him a sense of their peace and beauty.

But this serenity was banished when, a few minutes later, waiting at the post office for his turn at the delivery window, he heard voices behind the thin partition, familiar and girlish ones, and by-and-by his own name.

"Wherever did you get it, Dorothy, and whom are you going to send it to? It's lovely, and just barely in season."

It was Freda Colton's voice, shrill and eager, and a softer one answered, hesitating and reluctant, as if giving up some secret she would have kept, but could not:

"Uncle Ezra gave it to me. The wrapper to it was lost in the mail-bag, or else it was put in without any. Anyway, there was no address, and nothing with it to tell who sent it or where it came from, so it belonged to him, you know."

Ezra Given was postmaster at Oldberg, and Dorothy Carver was his niece. But the other's harsher tones broke in again:

"Well, it's a beauty, the handsomest one I ever saw, about. And that verse is lovely, too. Let me look at it again, will you? H'm! that wouldn't fit everyone, would it? Let me think, I should send it to Will Gushom."

Through the glass of some empty mail-boxes the listener could see the curl of the other's lip as she drew away, refolding carefully the valentine.

"They don't describe him," she said, simply, with a quick emphasis on the final pronoun.

"Fred Curtis, then?"

She shook her head again, and as decidedly at each name that followed.

"Ned Armstrong? Arthur Ellis? Frank Willman? Well, I give it up. You'll have to give it to John Bradley."

The honest sarcasm of the last words stung gentle, reserved Dorothy into unusual warmth and frankness.

"He *is* the only one they would fit, as you say," she replied, and holding the package tightly, she hurried away, glad to cool her hot cheeks in the frosty darkness.

And John Bradley, pocketing the Squire's mail mechanically, was glad of the shelter of the same cool shadows, and for once, of the long, lonely walk, albeit he was late already. Here was something to think of more absorbing, aye, and more satisfying than any problem that book-keeping or algebra or the fascinating geometry could furnish, or history suggest, though they had solaced many a lonely hour.

The Squire brought the mail himself the next night, throwing it on the table a little contemptuously as he entered.

"Nothing to speak of," he said, "but a letter for you, Mary, from Lois, I guess. The rest are circulars and papers. One of them is for you, John."

And, though his second glance at the brown envelope was a little keen, and was followed by a look at the youth himself, as with clumsy fingers he took it, he made no other comment, and John, thankful that Mrs. Patten had a few moments before complained of a whistling draft down the stairway, murmured something about his window's being open, and withdrew, mail in hand, ostensibly to shut it.

Once within the walls of his own room he drew a long breath that was almost a sigh, and opened the envelope with hands that trembled. He knew the handwriting in which it was addressed, and which there had been no attempt to disguise, and he knew by sight the folded missive that Dorothy had held so tightly twenty-four hours before.

There it was, in all its pristine daintiness, not a mark upon the glittering frost-work of its delicate decoration. And the verses that *she* had said fitted him. He bent his head to read them, and there is no honor that valor or nobleness can earn, or fellowman bestow, significant enough to make him so glad and proud as did that quaint verse from an old poet.

He sat quite still a long time after he had read it.

"Maybe it does, some of it," he said to him- -self, at length.

"It shall, anyway, sometime,. the whole of it."

Never was knightly vow made with fuller and more joyful consecration than this unwitnessed one. But of the endeavors that went to its fulfilment, homely, pathetic, persistent, self-forgetful, few knew, though all within the radius of his efforts were enriched, gladdened, or bettered thereby.

Oldbergians knew that Squire Patten hired him that spring and summer, but that he "kept himself awful close of an evenin', except it was conference or lecture, or something special at the town hall;" that he did the work of two with his young strength and tireless zeal. They knew he entered college in the fall, without conditions, and the Squire's nephew said the Squire had lent him, or offered to lend him, money enough to go through with. They knew he worked summers and taught winters, twice at Oldberg, where his success, measured by the solid acquirements of his pupils, and the inspiration and direction they somehow had from him, was something wonderful.

They knew that when Arthur Ellis was ex-
pelled in disgrace John was the only one who
stood by him or seemed to know how to win
his confidence, prevailing on the Squire himself to employ him as accountant in the office
at his own mill, and that it was doubtless
John's intervention—he had been three years
in college then—that saved two others of the
Oldberg boys from sharing Ellis's disgrace.
They knew he graduated with honor, took a
year at the Polytechnic, obtained at once a
position in some Western city, and, after the
briefest visit to his native town, during which
he took a decrepit great-aunt from the poor-
house, where she had been placed by some distant cousins whose unpaid servant she had been
through most of her active years, and placed
her in the family of widow Carleton, who would
care for her faithfully, and who was glad to
have the weekly addition to her income which
John pledged himself to make in payment.

There was, indeed, one person, yes, there
were two in the village who could have told
much more than this.   One was Squire Patten,
whose classmate, Judge Otis, was one of the
trustees of the college where John graduated,
and a resident of the college-town, who had
two cousins and more than one old friend

among the faculty, and was, though John never found it out, an uncle of the wife of the young president of the Polytechnic, and who, he was aware, though he seldom thought of it, had a somewhat abnormal faculty of eliciting information, which the informant was quite unaware of giving. But the Squire did not share his knowledge with his neighbors to any extent. They knew he had a good opinion of the young man, and declared he was "bound to win if only he didn't try to do too much for the other fellow," adding, though, with an inscrutable twinkle, that "John's judgment was pretty good for a young man, and he had made some splendid investments already," which remark set his neighbors to wondering if John could have accumulated anything so quickly, or if possibly the Squire had let him look after any of his stocks or bonds. They did not think of any other realm where money or strength or love might be funded. "Treasure in heaven," was a familiar phrase, indeed, but heaven as an actual place of deposit neither sermon, text nor life itself had ever suggested to them.

The other person to whom had come, more by intuition than by discovery, some real, continuous knowledge of John Bradley's life and what he was making out of it, and doing with it, was Dorothy Carver.   But she was more reticent than the Squire.   He wondered, indeed, whether she really knew more than he did, of what John was doing, or so much, sometimes ; and took pains to spend an evening occasionally at the Carvers', taking his wife and her knitting-work with him, that Mrs. Carver and she might chat together, and leave Dorothy free to listen, while he talked to her father, taking care to speak, meanwhile, in the course of the evening, of what was happening to Oldberg's sons and daughters at a distance, and telling most of the young men, and, whether he named him or not, of John.

And he was sure that whether the name was spoken or not, one hearer knew which story was of his quondam choreboy, which deed of modest heroism her old schoolmate had done, and which enconium, whether from his lips or only repeated by him, was bestowed on the man she and St. Valentine, all unconsciously, had knighted.

Dear, benignant, wise St. Valentine ! Does he make record of those who help keep his memory green, to return their offerings with interest?

Every year on the 14th of February, a package came to Dorothy, always addressed in the same hand, changing a little, but still firm, familiar and dear. Once it had been a box of exquisite violets; once royal-hearted pansies. Once it was a volume of noble poems, new then, familiar now. Once the latest thought of a gracious thinker, and once a lovely bit of landscape, that reminded both giver and recipient of the Oldberg woods.

So each year brought a tenderer thought, a more insistent suggestion. All that inanimate or growing things could tell, was told. Yet how little way their speech went after all!

Oldberg had by this time settled John Bradley's destiny to its own satisfaction. He was steadily advancing in his profession, was beginning to be called indeed "eminent" in it. His influence was felt too, along other lines. This Squire Patten corroborated.

Also he was to be married very soon to the daughter of one of his old teachers, now resident in the city where John was as one of the faculty of a new university. This the Squire corrected, not vehemently, but with sufficient decision, telling enough of John's habits, manner of life and plans, in Dorothy's hearing to assure her of its falsity. But the rumor lived, Protean-like, in Oldberg gossip still. Not even the Squire's denial could arrest it, nor did he seem to think it worth pursuing, as likely to be always foundationless.

The great aunt had died, and John had neither kith nor kin in Oldberg. He had not come for the summer visit the Squire and his wife hoped for, nor had he accepted their almost beseeching invitation to Thanksgiving. And so the old year grew late and faded away out of life, nay, left its life beyond it, out of which the new year would make what God willed.

In a box of peerless roses her friend had sent—for it was so she oftenest thought of him—had been a cutting which Dorothy had rooted and cared for till it became a thrifty rose tree. It lifted a creamy, half opened bud to her as she entered the sitting room one morning, and soothed her with its fine fragrance as she bent over it.

"I suppose I have my friend still," she said to herself, while a tear glistened on a green-veined leaf. "And after all, 'life holdeth no joy like a friend.' "

Her gladness warmed with the sunlight. It did not seem strange that no token appeared though the day grew late.

And when, at nightfall, after the last Western train had rumbled in, someone came up the path and in at the door, it hardly surprised her, nor was the voice strange to her.

"I have told all I could," it said. "You will have to say the rest—the answer to it."

A FLOWER MISSION.

The thought of it came while the March winds were sweeping through the Crofton hills. On Brier Hill was the little brown cottage where the flower missionary lived. So small and so high was it, and in summer so hung with vines, that when the leaves were grown you did not descry it till you were close upon it. And when the trees were bare, and the vines faded, the wee brown thing had the semblance of a gigantic bird's-nest. But it was not far, after all, from the little town; for Brier Hill rose abruptly from the village street. Crofton was far among the hills of a hilly New England region. Round about it were encircling hills, each a little higher than the one below it, till the outer circle pierced with its jagged cliffs the stainless azure, or seemed all the grander for the cloud and mist that half-veiled their majesty.

Delightful summers they had in Crofton, but all too short, set between the long, bleak, ever-threatening winters. The season had been, this year of which I write, unusually severe even for Crofton. Sick people suffered and died, and well ones fell ill, and were long in recovering. The Randalls, in the little, brown, Brier Hill farm-house, had had their turn. Ruth, the last to succumb, was slowest to recover. Indeed, they knew that health, if it came at all to her who had been last year so full of abounding vitality, could come only after months or years. Everyone's sunshine was dimmed with the knowledge. And she herself bemoaned the inaction that must follow, more than the suffering that went before. But one cheerless day, while they were yet snow-bound, her inspiration came.

The table was strewn with seedsmen's catalogues, and with old and new *Rurals* and *Agriculturists*, with the aid of which Father Randall was making up his seed order for the spring planting. Ruthie looked on listlessly, roused into interest only by the words of her mother, absorbed in papers of a different sort:

"Here is work for you, Ruthie! I wonder we haven't thought about it before. It's the Flower Mission. There's a piece about it here, and it reminded me of what your Cousin May told us last summer. Don't you know how sorry we were we hadn't anything to send, so to have a hand in the good work? You know she said they could make good use of many more than they had. Now you just try your hand at it; 'twill take you out doors and give you something to think about, and maybe do somebody else a good turn or two, as well."

"What's that, mother?" said the farmer, looking up.

"Oh! the Flower Mission, father, don't you know? They get together all the flowers they can, and carry them to poor people, and sick folks, and 'shut-ins,' and the poor little city children.

"We didn't begin in season last year, but this spring we can and will."

" 'Twill be the best medicine for you, childie," said the father, sighing as his eyes rested on the fragile form, the pale face, and the weak, thin hands, "and I'll help you."

"I'll have nice, old-fashioned flowers for part," she went on, eagerly, "pinks, and sweet william, and phlox, and marigolds, and such. Old people like them, and men and women knew and loved them as children, so they seem like old friends. And I'll send some wild flowers, too, if I can afford freight on so many. My pansies will do well this year, I guess; and the bulbs I planted last year will be in bloom. And I must make out a list of seeds and things for new ones too."

So the planning of this mission flower garden beguiled many weary hours. It was pleasant to send away an order, and receive the dozen or more little brown and blue packets, and pleasanter still to sow some ·in window-boxes, and watch their germination and growth. And when April slowly passed, and May came in, what joy to see the yellow "daffis" nodding in the wind, and the delicate wind-flowers budding in the breeze, and the crimson-vestured polyanthus standing prim and straight in the corner, and the pansies lifting their sweet faces in their tiny bed; and best of all, to cut and send away one small basket ere June had come! And following them, the lilacs and syringas, and tulips and jonquils and lilies-of-the-valley, all coming right along, as if eager to greet her, and help on her kindly plans.

This was while she could do no more than cut and arrange them; but as the days grew brighter, and strength began to return, she spent a part of every pleasant day among them, receiving infinite soothing and satisfaction, drinking in deep draughts of cheer and courage as she toiled among them. And like Shakespeare's "little candle," this "good deed," shining, sent its beams afar. Some unknown friend in the city hearing of her circumstances and efforts, sent a kind letter and generous check to further her schemes. The village paper found out what she was doing, and bethought itself to help in the work. They found out that, remote as they were, with modest incomes, and, of necessity, busy people, all, there yet were many things they could do to help and cheer their distant brethren and sisters toiling and suffering in circumstances more adverse. It paved the way for more substantial charities; the Fresh Air cause, the hospital charities, and others began to have supporters there among the hills; and the smypathies of Crofton people grew and strengthened as the summer waxed and waned.

The Minister (they spell it with a capital in Crofton) came one day to Brier Hill, finding Ruth in her garden.

"We didn't know what benevolent plans were developing in your brain when we were missing and pitying you last winter," he said, as he sat down in the shade. "Crofton begins to be proud of our philanthropist."

"Oh! Mr. Noble, don't laugh at me! I'm ashamed when people speak so! But it's all I can do just now, you know."

"My child, I am not laughing at you. You are doing real, gracious, blessed work, and I rejoice in it. It reaches farther than you dream of. And I know it is good for you, and helps you in many ways, does it not?"

"Oh, so much!"

"When your mother asked me last Sabbath for a copy of the sermon for you,—which I have brought to-day,—I told her you had sermons of your own every day, better than any of us can preach."

"The 'voiceless lips' do say a good many things that I never seemed to hear before."

"We are not always ready to hear," said the Minister, musingly.

"I wish," said Ruthie, "I could be sure that they say as much to those they are sent to. It would be better than the blossoms."

"Why don't you send the thoughts with them, at least sometimes?"

"Oh! it would be presumptuous, wouldn't it?"

"I don't think so."

"Then perhaps I could, occasionally, I'll think about it. It's queer, isn't it! Every now and then they make me think of some

Bible verse that perhaps I never thought much about before, and they make it all new and plain and very real to me. I should like to send those to some one that needs them."

"I would try it, if I were you," said the Minister, rising to join Mr. Randall in the strawberry bed, stopping to speak to the house-mother as he went.

And so Ruthie had another "idea," one she was not long in carrying out. After this, with every tiny basket, or carefully tied cluster of flowers, she laid a dainty card, bearing, sometimes with a blossoming spray painted upon it, sometimes in graceful Old English lettering, sometimes in plainest script, a Scripture text, one that had unfolded its meaning as she toiled over her flowers, or been suggested by something around them. Rarely, too, she put in another verse, full of significance or promise.

Those whose work it was to distribute them exercised rare tact in their work. Never preacher spoke to more attentive hearers, nor with finer discernment and fitness. To a poor old woman, looking back on disappointments and blighted hopes, feeling worn and broken, came a handful of dewy lilies with the promise, "I will be as the dew unto Israel." And into her sad soul stole a new, restful sense of God's own care and his fullness of tenderness, that effaced some overlaying dust of anxieties, and gave new life and freshness to the Christianity that was really hers. To a young girl, shut in a narrow room, whose only cheering outlook was one slender strip of sky, to whom came few ministers of consolation,—so few, indeed, that she hardly pined or looked for any,—was sent, with cool, delicious fruits and an illustrated book, a great cluster of rich verbenas with fresh, green leaves. And while she drank in beauty and perfume, and wondered at the unlooked-for joy that had come to her there fell out a card, declaring, "God is able to give thee much more than this."

A young man lay wasting with consumption in the wards of a great hospital, a believer, yet not freed from all the fear and dread of death. To his bedside was brought a great cluster of Ruthie's mission flowers, sprung from the seeds her hands had planted. And with these she had laid a card, bearing the thought they had illustrated for her.

"See" said the nurse, as she laid them in his hands, "flowers for you. And there's a card with some writing."

For some minutes the sick man lay caressing the blossoms. Many of them were like old friends. He had loved them long ago. By and by, as he turned, the card fell out with the text uppermost. Like the voice of an angel, like an echo of the divine comforting, seemed the words, "Not unclothed, but clothed upon."

In the next ward lay an older man, also sick with incurable disease, and slowly failing. With his boquet was the passage, "The flower fadeth, but the word of our God shall stand forever." To how many despondent hearts they brought home the truth of God's love and care, I know not. Only He keeps such records. But there must be many such. Now and then some cheering report of the good they did came back to the giver of the blossoms,—these I have mentioned and one other, a cripple, misshapen and maimed, and not yet led to serene acceptance of his life-burden by seeing God in it. With the blossoms, of many sorts and rare beauty, that were given him, were the words, "God giveth it a body as it hath pleased him." "I could believe it of them," he said, "an' as I sat a thinkin', it came to me that it is true for me too. And I can't begin to tell you how different it makes things. Tell them as sent 'em, I thank them heartily, an' always shall."

"And that," said Ruthie, "more than paid for all the trouble and care I'd taken, and would, if it had been a dozen times as much to do. Only" she added to herself, "it wasn't so much the flowers, as 'twas the 'wonderful words of life' that went with them. I am so glad I did it!"

9

A BELATED THANKSGIVING.

The November day, which had opened like June or September, serene and sunny, and sweet with lingering harvest scents, had become swiftly as dim and dreary as the grim month it belonged to had right to be. It was hardly later than mid-afternoon, by the village clocks —though to country-folk at this season, that is already "almost night"—yet the houses and hills in the distance began to look vague and indistinct, and the shadows were dark and heavy all around, as if it were really twilight.

"How fallish it seems?" said Mrs. Ellis. "I'm real glad I wore my woolen long-shawl instead of my Paisley, as I was a'most minded to. 'Twas so warm and pleasant when we started!"

"Yes, I don't know when we've had a prettier mornin'," rejoined Miss Cleaves.

"Seems' if 'twas going to snow right away," said Mrs. Gridley. The fourth occupant of the double-seated farm-wagon, jogging and

jerking along, in accordance with the unrhyth-
mic progress of a clumsy, not-to-be-hurried
gray horse, had no rejoinder ready to complete
this measure of the conversational quartet
which had gone on since they left the Corner.
She only looked, in a silence that seemed to
cover an anxiety, at the cold-looking fields,
bare now even of the stubble, at the gráy sky,
and at the little puddles over which the horse
stepped gingerly, and which were already
glossing over with a thin, brittle coat of
fragile ice, for the wind had grown very chilly.

"Seems real raw, don't it?" questioned Mrs.
Ellis. "Aint you cold, Mis' King? Here,
pull this buffalo robe over to your side.
There's plenty of it, only we've had more'n
our share. It's 'most Thanksgiving, aint it?
Comes early this year. I've just got my lard
tried out, and my head-cheese made. Henry,
he smoked the hams, good big cuts of 'em,
too. I told him I couldn't make sausage this
year, anyhow. Why, I aint got my mince-
meat done yet. I 'most generally have it out
of the way a good fortnight before Thanksgiving. And I expect his folks will be there,
too."

"Well, *I've* got to make a Thanksgiving this
year, whether I want to or not," said Mrs.

Gridley. "Sister Susan, she wrote that she was coming from Pennsylvania along the last o' the fall. She should get here by Thanksgiving, anyway. You know she aint eat a Thanksgiving dinner at the old home place in years and years! An' Jabez, her husband, you know, and probably one of my nieces, and maybe the two of 'em, will come with her. Martha Thorne's promised to help me some. Of course the boys will be at home, and Cora and her family. Her husband's just got home from Nebraska. They're terrible pleased!"

"Well, you have got a stent," said Miss Hannah Cleaves, "to do for so many! I don't hardly see how you will manage."

"There's a good deal in plannin'," remarked Mrs. Gridley. "I always do mean to be a little beforehand with my work, *especially* when there's company to do fer, or anything extry. I've got my mince all chopped, an' my sausage made, an' five loaves of pound-cake baked, besides my cleaning done up thorough," she added complacently, tucking the "buffalo" corner more closely around her.

"Well, I guess I shall jest shet up my house and go up to Alameda's Thanksgiving week," said Miss Cleaves. "She wants me to, an' I think likely 'twill be some help to her.

She aint real strong and the children can't
help much. They are all in school and Fanny's
only in her fourteenth year."

"My Mary's only a year older than that,"
said the woman who had been silent for a time,
"and she's a good deal of help now. Your
sister'll find her daughter will be by that time.
I declare, I shouldn't know how to keep house
without her."

"Your bein' alone makes a difference, I
s'pose," put in Mrs. Gridley, not heeding the
flush that spread, as she spoke, over Avis
King's usually pale face.

But Mrs. Ellis saw it, and hurried to salve
the wound by the first question that came to
mind. Perhaps she had even hoped to turn
the weapon, in that clumsy fashion we all have
of trying to arrest a sentence whose edge has
already gone to the quick with another glancing point of words. Perhaps the second,
coming where the hurt has been made already,
pains more than the first. It did in this case,
though she did not see it till it was too late.

"Are *you* goin' to make Thanksgiving this
year, Mis' King?"

"Why, I suppose I shall do something for
the children, you know. They always count
on it so much," Mrs. King stammered, flushing more deeply.

And Hannah Cleaves hastened to say :

"Of course they do, an' grown folks, too!
I remember one year, I wasn't very well, an'
I thought I wouldn't do anything, nor go anywheres, either, though Alameda and Ellen,
they both wanted me to. But my neuralgia
was bad, an' I hadn't any appetite, either, for
Thanksgiving, nor any other dinner. So I
told 'em I couldn't come, an' I sold my chickens, all of 'em alive, and got Job Rollins to
put in my squashes an' apples, an' things.
An' I thought what a nice time I'd have to get
rested, all by myself, an' so quiet there. I
could set 'round all day. Well, I *did* set
'round, and it *was* real quiet, only 'twas the
lonesomest kind of quiet, you *ever* saw. I
fairly got the blues, an' that's something I
don't often have! An' I said to myself, 'Hannah Cleaves, it serves you right, grumpin' off
by yourself the best day o' the year but one!
Stands to reason that thankfulness, the genuine sort, comes better where there's things going on, and folks to do for, if 'taint but little
—and to do fer you. The promise to two or
three is good for other times besides Sundays
and prayer-meetings. An' there's more'n one
or two you could have invited in, if you didn't
have all kinds an' a big dinner. 'Twould have

cheered 'em some, maybe. Another time you'll do different.' Oh, I just give it to myself. An' the more, because I *had* made half-a-dozen pies and sent 'em to one and another that was old and feeble, or hadn't much to do with. It made me think—my actions did, of something I read once in a piece of poetry; it was about it's not being what we give to folks, but what we share with 'em, that does 'em good. And the gift, without *us*, is bare enough. Doesn't sound very smooth, the way I tell it, but 'twas real poetry there."

"Mary's got the whole of that poem, you're thinking of, in a book her cousin Nora sent her; and it is beautiful," said Mrs. King. "You can take it sometime, if you want to," she added timidly. "I think you'd like to read the whole of it."

She had recovered her self-possession by this time, and, except that her voice was not quite clear, and her eyes brighter as if tears had been held back stoutly, she did not betray the fact that a very sensitive spot had been ruthlessly and carelessly touched. And her companions were as willing as she to pass over the inadvertence.

"There comes Zekle Nicholas with his everlasting peddle-cart," exclaimed Mrs. Ellis suddenly, as a forlorn looking team came in sight. "There, I can't help it," she added, slapping the horse with the reins, in a vain endeavor to hurry him. "Zekle is so slow an' putterin', an' so *dreadful* inquisitive! I get all out of patience with him. Now he'll stop an' quiz us half an hour, tryin' to find out where we've been. I guess the best way's to tell him now." So she accosted him at once:

"Chilly afternoon, ain't it, Mr. Nicholas? We've been over to the Forks to a Missionary circle, and to do some shoppin', too, and we're kind of late gettin' home. Folks all well, I s'pose? Ours is." By this time she had succeeded in persuading her horse to take three steps where he had taken only two before, and had urged him past the expectant Zekle. "*I* wa'n't goin' to have you all set there in the road a-shaking while he asked his forty-nine questions," she said triumphantly. "I tell you I've learnt to head him off when I can."

"They say his wife has got him into that way of doing," Miss Hannah said, apologetically. "Folks that know say she always asks him every time he comes home, who he's met, an' where they was goin', and what the folks where he'd called was doing, an' if the houses looked neat every time, and even what they

had for dinner or supper, if the table was set,
or what the women-folks was cookin', if 'twas
forenoon or a bakin' day. I s'pose she gets
lonesome, and I *have* heard wa'n't real bright."

"I've heard she was a real tattler, an' I guess
it's so," rejoined Mrs. Gridley with energy.
"An' I've known of a good many stories started
from that wa'n't no ways so. Well, here I am
at home again, an' ever an' ever so much
obliged to you, Mis' Ellis," she added, as the
driver drew rein before a white farmhouse.
"I'll have our horse some day when he ain't
quite so busy, to go somewhere. One good
turn deserves another, you know ! Good-night,
an' good-night again, Hannah ; an' Mis' King,
I'm comin' up to see you, an' bring my work,
just as soon as Thanksgiving's well over. I
know you're lonesome !"

Mrs. Ellis had already driven on, but her
voice, shrill and penetrant, carried her words
to them distinctly. No one seemed to have
anything to say, and they resumed the long
hill in silence. At its top, and a little way from
the road, stood a yellow house, at one of
whose windows a light shone feebly.

"I'd rather get out here. I've had a nice
ride, and a pleasant afternoon, and I thank
you. Come over and see me, won't you, and
you, too, Hannah."

"Just as soon as my company's come an' gone, an' I get righted round a little," said Mrs. Ellis, briskly. "I calculate on being pretty busy for two or three weeks, now. Can't you run in and see us while the folks are here? They'll want to see you."

"If I can, I will. Bring them over," said Mrs. King, raising her voice slightly, for the horse, impatient for his supper, was moving on. As she went up the little lane she could hear them talking still—for the wind had veered and bore their voices to her—Mrs. Ellis's quick, shrill tones contrasting oddly with the gentler, softer speech of her companion.

It was twilight now, and very shadowy under the eaves which sheltered the side door. She paused an instant, to look in. Mary had lighted a lamp in the kitchen and the little ones were gathered there.

Bennie, the studious, was perched at the table with a book before him. His blue eyes dilated as he turned eagerly the pages. Evidently it was some book new to him by his absorption, though one reading by no means exhausted the resources of any volume for him, and all the books and periodicals the house held were laid under tribute to his pleasure. Sober and earnest for his ten years, thoughtful, and with a mind seemingly athirst for truth, his mother oftened wondered how his growing longings and the ambitions already manifest, could be either satisfied or soothed. She sighed now as she watched him.

Nellie, his twin, her roguish eyes just now dreamy and still, sat on her cricket by the fire watching at a window opposite that into which her mother was looking, the reflection of the dancing flames outside the pane.

"Is it really the witches, I wonder, making their tea?" she asked. "Then I shall ask mother to have a very nice fire just at this time, one that will shine ever so bright out there. And one day I will watch and see them, and ask——"

"Ask what?" questioned Bennie.

"Ask them to do lots of things for us; to send father home, first of all, with a pocketful of gold."

But the other children interrupted her in almost scornful reproof.

"They couldn't do that if they was witches twice over," said Bennie. "Never!"

"Never, not any time, if they was witches really and truly," echoed little Sue, dancing back and forth between them.

"Nellie's forgotten what mother was telling her the other day, and she doesn't remember what we say 'Our Father' for," said May more gently.

"Didn't forget a single thing, so there! Maybe God would let the witches do it, and send 'em. Anyway, he made 'em, if there is any!"

"If!" said Bennie.

But they had no time to argue longer, for a door in the rear of the kitchen was opened, and a boy of thirteen came in with a pail of foaming milk. And at the same time their mother entered.

"Your milking all done, Fred? You're early to-night. And your supper smells good, May, after a ride in the cold. Did you change your shoes, Bennie? You know they leak. And what has mother's baby done to-day?"

"School was out early, and we came home around by Marcia's, and we went in there a minute. She had to go right home to help her mother. You didn't care?" said May. "She showed me a new lace she's doing, and lent me the pattern."

"I don't like to have you do so much of that," said her mother. "There's a book I borrowed for you in my satchel. Yes, I'll come to supper right away, just as soon as I can change my dress."

"Let mother warm her a little, can't you, and get rested," Fred said rebukingly. "There's no big hurry to-night."

"You're the very one that hurried."

"Well, I can wait," he answered.

"I was going over to Luther's," he said, when a few minutes later they were seated at the supper table. "The chores are all done, and I'll be back early. And, mother, wouldn't you be willing for me to ask him over to dinner with us Thanksgiving day? He's awfully lonesome."

"I'd be very willing, my boy, if we were going to *have* a Thanksgiving dinner."

"Aren't we?" Fred asked.

"Can't we manage and contrive somehow some other way," May asked regretfully, while the little ones stopped eating and looked up, round-eyed and sober.

"I don't see how we can," their mother answered, with a brave attempt at cheerfulness, "unless something very good should happen to us. I don't mean that we aint going to have anything to eat that day, but I'm afraid I can't afford to get a turkey, or even have a pair of our chickens. I want to get some coal within a few days for our sitting-room fire. We shouldn't want to do without that in these long evenings, when we're going to have such good times reading and studying and playing games." The children took it up.

"And popping corn," Sue said.

"And writing letters to father," added Nellie.

"And telling stories, and hearing 'em," put in Bennie.

But it was evident that they all were disappointed, and not even her recital of the afternoon's experiences could make them forget it.

Fred went out, but came back early. Bennie read till he was sent away with a good-night kiss, Sue crept into her mother's arms and fell asleep there, while Nellie dozed on the lounge, tired with the day's play.

They were all in bed at last, and Mrs. King locked her doors, drew her curtains closer, and drew up to the stove with her knitting, to face the thoughts that she knew must come sooner or later. The house grew still, so still that a cricket, which had been chirping by the chimney, hushed his song, as if oppressed by the lonesome quiet. Bruno, the dog, allowed to have his bed in the kitchen in the long nights for the protection his nearness gave, crouched soberly at her side, as if he understood that

she was far from glad. Indeed, her thoughts
were sad ones, and though her needles clicked
briskly, they were swifter yet. Back and
forth, round and round, with never a stitch
dropped in the stocking, and never a thread
broken or awry in the web memory was weav-
ing for her.

Five years before, when Sue was a baby
and Nellie and Bennie had hardly left babyhood behind them, her husband, discouraged
by the slow gains from the farm, anxious to
win a speedier and ampler competence than it
at best could yield him; above all, desirous of
providing for his children better opportunities
than he had had, or than he could by any possibility reach for them there, had joined the
company of fortune seekers always turning
westward. He had made all needed arrange-
ments for their comfort, had gone with good
courage, a confident hope of success, and had
promised to come home, whether successful or
not, within two or three years at longest. At
first, though the farm was lonely and her cares
many, it had not seemed hard. He had got
work at once, had written often, and had sent
money, which made the lessened income from
the farm of less consequence. But the remit-
tances had grown fewer, and for a long time

ceased altogether. He was ill, and unable to work for months afterward. Then he had sent a letter, telling of small investments he wanted to make with his earnings, and asking if she couldn't "manage,"—thrifty, pathetic, New England word, what unheralded heroism it covers! And now for some time he had sent small, infrequent sums, which barely sufficed to keep them all in comfort. For the family needs had grown and multiplied in inverse ratio to the contents of the family treasury. Her best foresight could secure only scanty revenues from the acres neither she nor her children could till. Meanwhile, their wants grew daily, and needs unfelt at first, or held in hopeful abeyance, grew urgent and clamorous. Fred and May were old enough, too, to use the privileges their father had meant to secure them. A little longer, and it would be too late to give them the fullest benefits. Nor was she certain that such comforts as they had would long be theirs, unless some help came.

Her purse held a trifle more than would buy a ton of coal. That she must have at once, and other dollars might come in before it was gone. The other things,—the coat Fred needed so, the dress she had meant May to have, Sue's cloak, and worst of all, Bennie's shoes, they must wait for. And they would have to do without their Thanksgiving dinner.

"And every one round will know it, children will tell things, and other children will inquire, if grown people don't, as very likely they will. And it gives them another thing to talk about, and makes them more certain that John has deserted us. And that is the worst and hardest of all! I can bear being poor, and having to scrimp and do without, but I am afraid I cannot bear having them say things. And they are beginning to say worse things, too," said this lonely woman to herself, dropping her knitting and sitting quite still. "I never would believe people thought such things, much less that they would hint them! Didn't I know what she meant when Maria Fitzgerald told all that stuff this afternoon? She didn't know whether I did or not,—I didn't *let* her. I don't see why they let her run on so—some one could have stopped her—unless they really wanted me to hear it all. What if some men have gone out there and drifted away from their families, and maybe forgotten they had any at all, all men don't! There's a difference, I'd have them know! And very likely it wasn't the same to begin with with them as with us. They needn't *imply* a comparison,

much less talk about desertions and—*divorce!*"
The last word came with a shudder, and in a
moment more she was sobbing bitterly. It
was for only a minute or two, though. She
quickly recovered herself, with only a little
longing cry of "Oh, John, John!" as if he
could hear and help.

Thanksgiving came that year in a dreary
week. It had been wet for days, and Thursday itself was drizzly and bleak. The King
children had accepted their disappointment,
and were trying to see what fun they could
have by themselves to make up for it. They
were not a little consoled when their mother
told them they might have a bit of candy-pull
at night or the next evening. And taken into
her confidence they were quite willing to help
her plan and economize, and make "the best of
things," a cheerful best.

"If only somebody don't come in that morning, or even at dinner time!" sighed May, who
loved to keep up appearances, "They do sometimes. On purpose to see, I do believe."

"Oh, no, they won't, unless it's Zekle, ped-
dling, and you don't care for him," said Fred
cheerfully.

"But I do," May protested, "and so does
mother. We'll set the table nice, and eat *just*
at noon. Most folks get home at that time."

But "Zekle" did not. They had just sat down when he came, and his small eyes saw in a moment all that was on their snowy tablecloth, as they knew. And they were aware that by to-morrow all their neighbors would have heard about it, with additions, inferences and variations. And the mother, at least, knew that it would furnish one more link to the chain of circumstantial evidence that supported their theory of the father's absence.

Perhaps it was for that reason, perhaps for others, that she stayed in quite closely for some days thereafter. Even the Indian summer weather could not tempt her farther than the end of the lane.

Fred and May went one still, mild afternoon to the village for the mail and to do other errands. They took Sue with them, and Bennie and Nell were spending the day with Miss Hannah. She loved children, and often had some little friend with her.

Left to herself, for she could not be persuaded to accompany the older children, and growing restless within the silent house, Mrs. King stepped out into the yard. Bruno was on the porch, and as she went by, he got up and sniffed uneasily, as if some one were about. And presently, in the lane, a man appeared.

"A tramp, very likely. But I'm not afraid, with Bruno," she said to herself. "I'm glad I fastened the door."

The stranger, if stranger it were, was walking very fast. Tramps do not often hurry. Perhaps it was—

"Why, John, John!"

He had indeed come, successful in a measure, and to stay.

"I only waited to get so I *could* stay," he said, as they sat together that night after the delighted children had at last been sent away. "And I should have come before, anyhow, if I'd realized about things. You ought to have told me."

"Why, there wasn't anything to tell," Avis said. Her eyes were very happy, and her hands lay folded idly in her lap. The house was warm and still. The fragrance of her plants came from the stand by the window, where the moonlight, almost as bright as the lamplight, came between their leaves and lay in little odd patches of shadow on the floor in the corner. A cricket—was it the same one? —was chirping happily beside the chimney.

So they had their Thankskiging—for the children remembered the feast denied them— a day of good cheer, of merriment, of deep, grateful content. And once more "Zekle" opened the door as they sat at table. He had not heard the news.

"Oh, got company, have ye?" he said, confusedly, but still cunningly, noting the holiday dainties. "Why, it's Mr. King, I declare. Well, well! And I guess your folks is glad! Looks like Thanksgiving day here now, I'm sure."

"It is," said Avis quietly. No curious comment could pain her now. "Ours was belated."

LUTHER'S INHERITANCE.

The Hathorn homestead was the barest and dreariest of all the farmhouses in the region. Its plainness, too, was made more striking by the absolute neatness that characterized the premises. Its wide door-yard was swept clean, its wood-pile, on the left, was primly square, and not a chip or broken shingle dared to stray from the neighborhood of the weather-beaten, battered chopping-block.

There was never a flower-bed underneath the windows, nor even a rose-bush whose blossoms could scatter their petals on the gravel-less walk. The mistress of the house did not love such things. There was only a tall cluster of lilac-bushes half-way down to the road, and two or three ancient apple-trees near the well.

The unshaded house had never been painted. It stood on a tiny elevation surrounded by fields that looked as if they had little to yield their owner, save a scanty hay-crop, or some bushels of corn, though in one corner a garden showed its carefully kept rows, and a bit of a strawberry-bed displayed thrifty runners.

The barn, a long, low, dingy structure, was opposite the house. Behind it a wide pasture stretched, green and inviting despite its rockiness. Through the lane that led to it there filed, night and morning, a little herd of cows, well-fed, sleek, and gentle. They were the dependence of the family, and Mrs. Hathorn's butter was famous for its excellence. It was the thing she prided herself on ; one of the few things she could do. Therefore, with much firmness, she refused to consent to merging the little dairy into a milk-route. A venture, at best ; besides, they couldn't start out in it without running in debt, and that she would not do.

This had been, as it were, the key-note of her hard, toilsome life. By dint of continuous industry, of the most careful economy, and with deprivation of much that makes life sweet, they could win a maintenance from their rocky acres ; could have food, and shelter, and lights, and such plain clothing as was necessary, and for it all owe nothing. So they had kept on in the old routine, mother and son, these many years. There had been other children in the family, but they had died of a neighborhood epidemic in their childhood, and the father had shortly followed them. Luther, the youngest, and in many respects the least promising, was the only one left. A stolid, shy, spare young man, who submitted for the most part to his mother's plans and followed the guidance of her management in all the work of the farm, yet who had ambitions of his own, and periodical discontents with the standing order of things.

He had wanted to try market-gardening, but she dreaded the possible failure in it. He had longed for a milk-wagon and the belongings, that he might relieve her of her heaviest tasks. He had talked of opening a small quarry that showed its stony head in the farther pasture ; but all of these meant risk, and Mrs. Hathorn would not agree to them.

"We've always lived honest, and paid our debts as we made 'em, and had a comfortable living, so's we could ask a stranger to a meal any time, or have our relations come. I think 'twould kill me if we owed anybody and couldn't pay 'em, or if the place had to be mortgaged or anything. I think we'd better keep right along, Luther."

And Luther would yield a silent unsmiling submission, and would not harness his gray horse to drive over on the west road of an evening for a week thereafter. It was on the west road that Mary Donaldson lived. They had been nearer neighbors once, and he had used to draw her on his clumsy sled to and from the schoolhouse in the winter weather, when both were little children. She taught the district school herself now.

On this June day, when my story commences, Luther, going into dinner, could see across lots and discern with his strong young eyes, a slim, brown figure surmounted by a white shade hat, and followed closely by smaller figures in pink and blue and grey, getting, all of them, as near as they could to "the teacher," hurrying along the roadside, eager to make the most of the brief morning.

It was not of this that he spoke, however, as they ate.

"Simms' folks are having a piazza put on, I guess. And I do believe Miss Trotter's having her house painted. How much knitting would it take, do you suppose? 'Taint bigger than a bandbox."

"Jotham Simms is in debt for the lumber his barn is built of, now, that new one," rejoined

Mrs. Hathorn, quickly. "And his own cousin, that's sick with consumption, came there last week, thinkin' to stop a spell and visit, and he was shown so plain that he wa'n't welcome that he took the stage the next day for the Corners, where there's an aunt of his lives. And he and Jotham was brought up together, like own brothers, too. I tell you, Luther, things aint always just as they seem to be."

"I could paint this house," volunteered Luther, now the ice was broken, "and the paint couldn't cost much."

"'Twould be something. And when we'd begun, we'd want to do something, and a good many somethings, inside," and she glanced around the room wistfully. "I don't like the look of things any better than you do, but I guess we'd better wait. Cyrus Lane may take the corner wood-lot. That would put us in as good shape as anybody round."

But Luther shook his head dubiously. That bit of purchase had been discussed too long for him to have any hope of its speedy consummation.

"I'm going over in the further pasture mending fence. If you want me you can ring the big bell. I sha'n't probably be back till supper-time," he said, having finished his dinner, stroked the black cat, and filled the wood-box.

"I sha'n't want you, I don't imagine. But if I was you I'd come home early, and do the chores in middlin' season. It's meeting-night at the school-house, you know, and I thought we'd go, if I don't get too tired."

She watched him as he strode off down the lane, noticing that he was not whistling as usual, and that Bowser, the dog, trotting along by his side, did not get even a word of recognition, and she sighed over her dishes, glancing around, as she put them in their places in the tall corner cupboard, to see again how plain and homely the rooms were.

"If there was any way I *could* do anything! But I truly don't see as there is. The butter-money just keeps us along. I don't doubt maybe Luther would make more some other way, but it's the getting into it that costs. I didn't tell him, but I had three-quarters enough to buy a milk-wagon saved out of the fleece-money and the pop-corn he laughed at, and half of it went to old Aunt Nancy when she broke her leg, and it took the other half to make us whole when Cynthia and her children came last summer. Poor, little peaked things, I declare I don't know which looked most helpless, she or the young ones. And he said

as well as me, that we couldn't let 'em go back
under a month.　And four extra in your family *does* make a difference, if they *are* own
folks and you don't have to make much change
for 'em.　If I'd had a little to do with, then,
Cythy'd have taken hold and helped me fix
up here; but 'twa'n't no use then.　I couldn't
spare a cent.　And I believe it looks worse
than it did then."

She tapped disconsolately, with the toe of
her coarse, worn shoe, the unpainted floor,
white as frequent scrubbings could make it,
but worn and slivered by years of wear.
There were green paper curtains at the windows, made necessary by the absence of blinds.
An oilcloth cover was on one table, and the
snowy table-cloth was still on the other.　The
stove was clean and shining, and there was no
dust nor litter anywhere, but the utter absence
of ornament and even of all attempts at beauty
was the more striking in contrast with the
loveliness outside.

On the other side of the narrow entry, a half
open door revealed a room, only less bare.
Here, the floor was painted, and there was a
crimson table-cover on a square stand, and a
patch-work cushion in the rocking-chair.　It
had a tidy on it, too, this chair, which Mary

Donaldson had given one Christmas. Mrs. Hathorn noticed as she passed the door on an errand into the entry that the tidy was sideways, and that there was a thin layer of dust on the album that lay on the table. Going in to right these matters, she stopped a moment by the west window to adjust the curtains, and looked out in the same direction that her son's eyes had wandered.

" 'Tis hard for Luther!" she said all to herself. "He'd have brought a wife here five years ago, if 'twas a home to bring her to. And Mary's a good, faithful girl. I haint got a mite o' fault to find with her. And I don't doubt, with the knack she has, and the things she's got ready, and what she's got saved, she'd make a very different place of it in a very little while. It's her way, and her mother's way. Their sittin'-room's as homelike and pleasant as can be, without very much in it either. If one of my girls had lived, p'raps I'd have had more faculty as well's more courage about things," and a tear or two rose in the grey eyes and rolled down the wrinkled cheek. She wiped them hastily away, however, with one corner of her gingham apron, and went on with her soliloquy. "And I don't know, sometimes, but 'twould pay, if it *was* a

venture.   Maybe a man has better courage with
a cheerful, homelike place to come to when
his day's work's done.   Luther's trusty and
steady at his task, but there is folks gets on
faster.   Though, poor boy, if he had what be-
longs to him there wouldn't be any need of
his slavin' nor stintin'.   That *was* the queerest
mess! I think likely a law-suit would have won
it, but I wouldn't favor it, against his own
father's brothers, too.   Let 'em keep it if they've
a mind to.   We can get along without it.   And
I wouldn't swap my conscience for Silas
Hathorn's, for he's at the head and foot of it,
being the oldest, and a good deal stronger
willed than Ephraim.   I haint seen either on
'em for twenty years, not since Enoch was
buried.   And I sha'n't ever be likely to.   If
they wouldn't take notice when Luther was little, and me a-having a hard time to face things,
why of course they won't now.   But just a
little money,—a few hundreds where they've
got thousands,—would make this world such a
different place to Luther.   He'd have a home,
then! I don't care so much for myself.   I'm
hardened to it, I guess," and the honest lips,
which never could be unkindly, no matter how
much sorrow or anxiety or disappointment
they had shut into her patient heart, refusing

to complain,—parted now in a broad, pitying smile. "But I don't see," she added, "how it can be helped, not just now!"

It was not ten minutes later that wheels sounded in the yard, and Mrs. Hathorn, opening the door, saw an old-fashioned, dusty wagon, with a robe laid on the back of the seat, country fashion. In it sat a withered looking old man, thin and brown, but with piercing dark eyes under his gray, shaggy lashes. The hands that held the reins looked weak and tremulous, too feeble, Mrs. Hathorn thought, to guide the strong, young horse.

"What can I do for you, sir? she asked, stepping out on the door-stone.

"Nothing, nothing—unless you give me a drink of water here. My colt is restless, and I don't like to leave him. I had my lunch down beside the spring here, and not being able to get out to get a drink with it, I'm rather thirsty."

"My son should hold him, and let you get out and rest," she said, "if he was round home this afternoon. You look beat out."

"A little tired, that's all, he answered, as he drank the milk she brought out with the asked for water. "I've ridden quite a good bit to-day, more than I'm used to. And I'd forgotten these roads were so ledgy."

"Somebody that knows the place," thought Mrs. Hathorn, as she took back her glasses. "But I can't place him anywheres. May have been before I came here; he looks old enough. But if 'twas my folks, I wouldn't let him ride 'round alone with that colt prancing and skittish, and them thin, tremblin' hands! It aint safe. And how sharp he does look at anybody. I'd be almost afraid if he didn't seem so old and feeble."

"Won't you sit and rest awhile," she asked, coming to the door again "It's shady, this side of the house, after dinner. May be your horse will stand."

"No, I thank ye," he answered, and she noticed that his quavering voice had a familiar ring to it. "No, thank ye, I guess I must go on. Good day, ma'am!" and he bowed courteously as he drove off.

Half an hour later she sat at her window with some mending in her lap, and started at the sound of voices and of hurrying feet at her door. Some one had been hurt, they were bringing him in. Of course it was Luther.

"No, it isn't Luther, Mrs. Hathorn. It's an old man got thrown out down the road here, and got hurt a little. I think he's broken his ankle, but he sticks to it it's only a sprain. A stranger, ain't he? Anyway, he is to us, but he wouldn't let us carry him into Grafton's—it happened just a little way below there—but made us bring him up here. And where'll we put him?"

Of course Mrs. Hathorn's spare bed-room was opened, the curtains tied up hurriedly, and the blue and white spread turned down from the comfortable-looking bed.

"I don't know him from Adam," she was explaining, excitedly. "He came along here a little while ago and wanted a drink. I thought that horse was too smart for him. And does anybody know who his folks are?"

This inquiry was made, of course, out of hearing of the injured stranger; nobody could answer it, nor was it answered for a long time thereafter. The injury proved rather a serious one, especially to be sustained by so old a man.

"For," said Mrs. Hathorn, "I don't believe he's a day under seventy, and I'd be willing to put five or ten years on to that. It'll make your work harder, Luther, this time 'o year, too, but there's no help for it. He don't look to me like a poor man, and he'll most likely be able to pay for staying here, if not for the care. And if he *was* poor," she declared with vehement and generous energy, "and couldn't pay a cent, why, I'd keep him all the quicker. I do feel a little worried, though," she added, "about the doctor's bill.   That leg will have to be attended to, right along, for some time now, and I s'pose I will be responsible."

But her anxiety was lessened that very evening by seeing their visitor himself pay the physician for his services when the latter left him, a practice which he followed at every subsequent visit.   The old leathern wallet from which he took the money was singularly gaunt in its appearance.   And, though payment was always forthcoming for the few medicines he needed, and for whatever his condition rendered necessary, he never indulged in any luxuries, nor seemed to crave anything beyond the simple fare that Mrs. Hathorn provided for him.

He lay quite patiently on his bed while the bone was knitting, yet seemed as pleased as a child when he could be lifted to the lounge, and, a little later, occupy the great rocking-chair in the family room.   Here, by the east window, that looked out over pleasant fields and pasture lands to the low hills of the sun rising, he would sit, strangely content, day after day.

Mrs. Hathorn used to beg him to sit in the other room.

"It's cooler there, and fixed up to be a little more seemly," she would say. "You must be tired of this homely place. Now do let me move your chair in there."

"No, no," he would answer, "I like this best."

"I've meant this dozen years to have things different," she went on. "And maybe I shall get to it sometime. I like the place because my husband brought me here when we were married. And some of his folks had lived here for I don't know how long before that. They moved away about that time, over east here, somewhere near where you came from, I shouldn't wonder. Hathorn, the name is, and they all descended from Jabez Hathorn; that was my husband's father's name, too."

But the old man did not seem inclined to talk about his neighbors, if, indeed, any of the Hathorns were among them, nor did he ask many questions, though he noticed curiously every detail of the family life. He was delighted when one afternoon Mary Donaldson came over and brought him a cluster of small, spicy pinks tied up with a bit of southernwood.

"There was a root of that here, once," said Mrs. Hathorn, "yes, and of the southernwood, too. But you know I'm no hand with flowers, and I believe they both died, long ago. 'Twas just in that corner by the front door that the pink root was," pointing out where, indeed, the man's eyes seemed to have been turned before. "I'd like to go out a little while," she went on, "so if you don't mind, I'll get Mary to sit with you, Mr. Tullock."

"What did you say? Oh, certainly, certainly. I shouldn't mind being alone here," he answered.

And though he enjoyed the afternoon with his young guest, he seemed either anxious lest Mrs. Hathorn should stay in too closely, or a little disturbed by their careful surveillance, and both he and they were glad as the injured limb grew daily stronger, and the days of his confinement fewer. He was evidently not a demonstrative person, and Mrs. Hathorn was not surprised or disturbed because, when he left them, his thanks, though warm and hearty, were few and somewhat constrained.

"Poor old man," she said, "I should like to know what sort of a home he's got, to like this place so well. For he did like it, and hate to leave someway. I found him crying at that east window this morning. Of course I didn't let him know I saw. I'm going to inquire of Cynthy. Tullock—I believe that was the name of your father's grandmother, Luther."

"That valise that had the name on it might have belonged to her," said Luther, irreverently. It was in this way that they had learned their visitor's name. "'Twas old enough, I'm sure."

It was in the evening of the day on which the old man had gone, and the young man was in excellent spirits. Mr. Tullock had paid well for board and care for himself and his horse. And indeed it was not often they had had a sum so large as this modest amount.

"It's as good as summer boarders," said Mrs. Hathorn, "and I never could take them on account of the house."

One of the first things planned was the painting of the house. And before the first coat was fairly dry, a letter came to Luther, which contained important news. His share of the property of his grandfather, it stated, having awaited certain formalities of law, was now at his disposal. It was necessary only for him to prove his identity at Hayford bank, where the amount was now deposited.

Of course changes came fast and thick thereafter, and the Hathorn farmhouse suffered transformation at once.

"I hate to have the old place changed, after all," said Mrs. Hathorn. "'Twon't ever seem the same, of course. But there, I've had my home in it as it was, and my life. And if Luther and Mary's going to have theirs together, I think it's time they begun."

This was to cousin Cynthia, who was making a little visit in early September, helping Mrs. Hathorn move and make and plan, as the bare old house was made to take on a new aspect. She was coming again by and by, for the wedding.

"I suppose," she said, "Cousin Silas will be here. Though you haven't told me you liked him."

"Silas who?"

"Why, Silas Hathorn, of course."

"I haven't seen the man for over twenty years," said Mrs. Hathorn.

Cynthia laughed merrily.

"Except when you took care of him, when he was thrown out and hurt here, at your door."

Mrs. Hathorn stood bewildered. "I do believe it was, and I might have known," she said. "But I truly never knew it, Cynthy."

"He said you didn't, and he liked it all the better. He was so pleased to think you should pick up that name off the old valise and tack it on him! But, don't you know, that's where Luther's property comes from."

"When we was married," put in Mrs. Hathorn, "my husband's father moved off this home place and give it to us. And he took his two other boys and moved over east here, where he had another farm, ever so much better, and some mill property, and I guess some land besides. He said we should have our share, just the same. And he did well over there. But he died sudden, and things was mixed up, and a good deal of the property in Silas's name, and nothing ever came to us at all. And I wouldn't fight for it, nor even ask. Here we was, and they knew it. But what started Silas out?"

"Why" replied Cynthia, "I don't hardly know what 'twas at first. He took a notion he'd ride over this way and see how you was situated. You know he wanted Ephraim's children to have it, he thinks so much of 'em. But I suppese his mind wasn't quite easy. And then coming here, and being sick, and sitting there by that east window in his mother's chair—oh, he told me all about it when I was over that way this summer—it made him think maybe that Luther's as near of kin as anybody.   For you know he put on quite a slice out of his own share, to make things even, he said."

"No," said Mrs. Hathorn, "I didn't know that.   I thought 'twas just in the straight line of inheritance.   But I ain't sorry, I think Luther and Mary will make a good use of it."

"That's just what he thought," said Cousin Cynthia.

ABNER'S WAY.

"I don't care! It is mean for Uncle to be so stingy! There, I've said it if I didn't mean to. And what else is it? We haven't had a regular Thanksgiving since I can remember. Never had anybody, more than Aunt Nancy or Grandma Carr, in all these years; and I did think maybe we could this year. But, of course, they won't think of such a thing, and wouldn't do it if they did!"

She sat on the cellar stairs, this tearful, indignant maiden — Nannie Holcomb, one Monday morning in November. It was a bright, bracing day, and some small rays of sunshine penetrated even the cellar's semi-darkness. One particularly lively sunbeam— its capricious course determined by the fluttering clothes on the dryer outside, went dancing up and down among the bins and barrels as if to inspect their contents, or, more likely, in a kind of sunny ecstasy over the harvest wealth therein displayed. And, in truth, there was good reason for exultation, or as grieving Nanny thought, thanksgiving. There were long bins of potatoes, sound, shapely, sizable; barrels of apples, red and gold and russet; boxes of beets, showing their ruddy skins through clinging soil, and big, dull-colored turnips. There were great heaps of golden pumpkins shining in the gloom like globes of solidified sunshine, and smaller piles of winter squashes of paler tints and lesser size. There were baskets of late pears in the warmest corner, and boxes with suspicious coverings whence came a fragrance as of grapes. Through the gauzy doors of a swinging cupboard might be seen the golden balls of the last churning, and by their side, on a long tray, were combs dripping with translucent honey.

"Enough here, anybody would think, to keep Thanksgiving with," went on the girl, "only 'twould be like the play of Hamlet with Hamlet left out, for I don't believe Uncle Enos has saved out any turkey; and I should think he might!"

And the girl lost herself in regretful reverie once more. She was a pretty girl, this little Nannie, though the small hands were a trifle red with much housework, the soft brown hair blown into tangled waves by the wind as she had gone in and out, the fair cheeks tear-stained now, and the brown eyes red with crying. Enos Carr had taken her into his heart and home in her desolate, orphaned babyhood. Very comfortable she had found the latter, all these twenty years, despite its sober quietness. Very pleasant it had been to grow up in it, to assume one by one little housewifely cares, as a daughter might, and finally to find herself mistress, with undisputed sway over all things in-doors, and not a little influence in out-door affairs. Yes, the home was certainly a dear and pleasant one. She loved it well. And Uncle Enos's heart—well, it seemed to her a good one in its way. He cared for her, of course, in his own staid fashion. She did not think it was in Uncle Enos to love anyone very enthusiastically, perhaps. And Abner was as like him in most ways as son could be like father. Abner was younger and quicker to comprehend, of course. He had his own ways, quite unlike those of any other whom Nannie had ever seen. He was very thoughtful of her comfort; very careful that she should not overwork. He studied with her, history and literature and botany and mineralogy and music. He read the papers to her, and talked over their contents. He helped her care for her plants, and got her new, rare ones. He brought her dainty trifles, new music and late books, whenever he went to town. Nannie did not like to think what life might be without Abner—he was so good and kind and cousinly, though he wasn't really her cousin, nor a relative at all. He was Uncle Enos's son by his first wife; she, the niece of the second Mrs. Carr.

It was funny, Nannie mused, that Abner didn't think they ought to keep Thanksgiving by having their relatives with them. There were just three or four families who would make such a nice little company. Aunt Nancy and Uncle and Aunt Guyson, with Nell and Frank, and Aunt Kate and Ned. Ned was home this year, which didn't happen always, and he would come of course. Nannie knew he would be glad to, for he had walked home from church with her only the night before, and he had said that the country was lonely, or that their farm was. He hoped it might not always be.

Nannie had not cared to consider what he meant, but she would have liked him to come to their house for Thanksgiving. That would make things a little less lonesome for him.

There were steps and voices outside, and Nannie remembered in a panic that the rollway was open. She would have fled upstairs, but she caught the mention of her name. It was Abner's voice first:

"Good weather for Thanksgiving, isn't it, if it only holds. Father, I don't know but we ought to invite the folks over, and make Thanksgiving ourselves this year, Uncle Joe had us all last year, and it's our turn, and I think Nannie would like it."

"She hasn't said anything about it to me. I thought maybe 'twould make too many chores for her," returned the elder man.

"No, nor to me, but I think she'd like it, and I don't believe she'd mind the extra work."

"Might ask her, anyway," said Uncle Enos. "Well, I'd like to see our folks together again, I believe, what's left, after all, and at my own table, too. And maybe it is dull for Nannie sometimes, though you seem to do what you can for her, Abner."

What Abner said Nannie never knew. She took advantage of the clock's striking to run away upstairs. She was not surprised when Uncle Enos proposed, at noon, a Thanksgiving family party, and she assented very readily, declaring, as Abner had foreseen, that she shouldn't mind the work, especially with Ann Chantry to help during the days that intervened.

She was surprised, however, at Abner's thoughtful kindness for her, used as she was to it. She wondered anew at the ways he found to help her. She set it down once more to "Abner's way." For that "way" included, she had found, a marvellous, protecting tenderness, as unobtrusive as sunshine. It was very good in a busy time, too. And on the strength of it she allowed herself to be persuaded to go with Uncle Enos next morning to invite their guests. It was a delightful drive, and Uncle Enos was the best of company. If she had ever thought him cold or distant she forgot it that day. Once only he pained her.

"I suppose it is lonely for young folks here at the farm," he said, "and especially women-folk. We're so contented always, Nannie, we haven't thought, or I haven't, that you might be getting lonely. You could go to the city for a good long visit this winter. Your Aunt Letty would delight to have you with her; and you could go to school then, if you like, or anywhere else."

But Nannie cried out against it. Kind as the words were, they somehow hurt her cruelly.

Didn't she belong at the farm? Leaving it or them had not entered her mind. Was not her place there with them? She did not say this, of course, but her heart was sore at the thought.

Their friends were easily persuaded to come for Thanksgiving dinner with them at the farm. Ned and his mother lived on another road, and were last to be visited. It was ten o'clock as they drove up the lane.

"I'm terrible thirsty," said Uncle Enos, as he returned his massive silver watch to his pocket. "If you don't mind sitting in the wagon a few minutes, there's a cold spring over here in the meadow that I'd like to get a drink from, as I used to when I was a boy. We're so near the house you won't be afraid, and you can go in without me if you will."

But Nannie would rather stay in the wagon. They had come by a way that was little travelled, and had stopped on a side of the house that was little used, save that an outer kitchen, which Aunt Kate seemed not yet to have abandoned for warmer winter quarters, was on that side. It had no windows looking in that direction, however. It was unfinished, and the loosely fitted boards of its rough walls—it was a "lean-to"—let out the odors of the morning's cooking, and the sound of voices as well. They were distant and indistinguishable at first, but soon a voice that she knew, questioned with masculine impatience:

"Breakfast ready?"

"As soon as I get the butter and cream. I've kept things hot for you, and'll have 'em on in a minute. I didn't know just when you'd be down. I knew you'd be tired after yesterday's hunting."

The last words were almost lost in a vanishing diminuendo as the speaker evidently hurried away to milk-room and pantry for the missing articles.

"No steak, of course!" grumbled the masculine voice again. Was this Ned's way? "You might try to have something decent, seems to me. I aint here every day."

"There's cold meat and an omelette. I didn't know you'd care." Then even more timidly, "You're not going out to-day, are you?"

"I'm off for town at noon. Shan't be back till the last train comes to-night. What's up now?"

"Nothing, only I wanted you to see Lawyer Pratt about those notes, and we've got to have another deed made out, of the south meadow, that your father bought of Jones, you know. They've straightened the road and made changes around. And I thought maybe we could go over to the graveyard."

"Bother! I shan't go there, anyway. The other things can wait. Or maybe you can attend to 'em. I don't see why not."

Nannie did not catch the whole of the mother's complaining protest of rheumatic pains, of work at home, of inability to comprehend and arrange those business matters, and dislike to attempt it, for Uncle Enos came back just then, and they went around to the side-door and went in. Nannie more than suspected that Ned had not finished his breakfast, but his manner betrayed no embarrassment of interruption. He was as attentive and genial as ever. If she could have but forgotten that just-heard conversation, it would have been a pleasant call. As it was Ned found it hard to account for her sudden coldness, and wondered why, if she cared so little, she took the trouble to invite them at all, or even to accompany Uncle Enos. But they accepted the invitation notwithstanding.

What a pleasure after that to go back to the farm! to find Abner waiting to welcome them with cheery words, which were no pretence, since with them, Nannie well knew, both thought and deed accorded; to find Ann Chantry, on

11

whom the neighborhood relied for help in emergencies, there at work already, and the day's work well under way. Just enough had been done to materially lighten Nannie's burdens, yet not enough to seem to encroach upon her authority as mistress of affairs. It was always so. That, too, was one of Abner's ways. And there came a sudden consciousness of his goodness—of his instinctive divination of her thought and mood and liking, and provision for them all—and of all the silent tenderness which had wrapped her like an atmosphere these many years, of which, because of its very naturalness, she had been unmindful. Whether it was his way toward all womankind, or whether there was in it something kept for her only, Nannie did not try to determine.

The next two days were very happy ones; so cheery, somehow, that Nannie wondered if Thanksgiving itself would be any brighter; and she questioned if, after all, the day would not have been pleasanter spent just by themselves—though perhaps they ought to have their relatives—and said as much to Abner, who answered a little surprised:

"I did think so at first, for Father's sake. It reminds him so of Mother, you know," he said, gently. "It was their wedding day, and she died, too, at Thanksgiving time. But I think he was willing to have the folks this year," he concluded more cheerfully.

"Oh, Abner! I never knew it!"

It was all she could say, and he bade her not to mind. But she was hurt and pained and sorry and ashamed all at once. That was the reason, then, why they never kept Thanksgiving with very noisy gladness. And she had thought them hard and close and unfeeling. Could she ever make up for it? She would try, and all her life, if they would let her. Of course she could not say this to Abner— then. There came a time when she could and did, for he asked her something very like it. It was weeks afterward, to be sure, but this Thanksgiving time helped to hasten it; for it was a very cheery Thanksgiving party. All the guests enjoyed it, none more, however, than the three who were not guests, but hosts and hostess. Perhaps it needed just the presence of strangers to show them how much they were to each other. For it was but a little later, as I said, that it was decided that nothing but death should part them—these three. Of course the vows to that effect were to be given and taken by only two of the household, but the father seemed, somehow, a party to the compact. It was his gain and joy, too, he said. Perhaps it was because the younger man, despite his proud consciousness of ownership, was so generous in his love. For this, too, was Abner's Way.

HER GIFTS.

The late March sunshine, reflected from acres of glittering crust, lay in warm lines along the yellow floor of a long many-windowed kitchen. The air within was spicy with scents of the Saturday baking, sweet with the odor from a kettle of bubbling sap fast changing to maple syrup, and made fresh and woodsy by a little breeze that came in through the open pantry window looking out into the wood-yard.

The mistress of the kitchen and of the farmhouse itself, though her authority was so mild and unobtrusive that you would hardly think of giving her the title, stood at her plant-stand, watering-pot in hand.

She performed her task with loving faithfulness, but there was an absent look in her eyes as she wiped the ivy leaves, blew some imaginary dust from the opening calla, and pinched the yellowing leaves from the sturdy lemon geranium. And it was almost mechanically that she bent to examine the tiny shoots of the early tomatoes and cucumbers in the long window boxes.

"Doing well, all of them," she said, in the tone of one used to having herself for sole listener. "Let me see, 'twas the first day of the month I planted 'em. Yes, they have grown amazingly. To-day's only—why," with a glance at the calendar—"it's the eighteenth. Just a week more !"

The preoccupied look was gone now.

"I believe," she went on, "I'll sweep them two back chambers to-day, and be that much beforehand. I shall have just about time enough before dinner. There's two pies in the oven I shall have to take out, though, before I go up chamber. Well, then !"

She gave a peep at the slowly browning pies, then turned to a tall cupboard in the corner and took down a great china bowl quaintly flowered. This she set carefully down upon the table, which was partially spread for dinner, and seated herself before it, drawing towards her, as she did so, the sugar-bowl. She then measured out carefully twenty-one teaspoonfuls of sugar, which she put into the flowered bowl, looking into it with satisfaction as she did so.

"I might have taken a tea-cup and saved time," she said, "but it seems a little honester to take it out with the teaspoon just as if I wanted it for my tea. And I needn't have stinted myself to get it, either, I don't s'pose. Likely enough Asa would ha' been willing as willing. But I don't want to make an offering of other folks's things, especially when its unbeknownst to 'em; and it hain't hurt me, a woman of sixty-five, to drink my tea without sweetening for a spell. I won't pretend I like it better so, but I'm glad I done it. There, that makes eight cupfuls, sure, and the butter's mine without reckonin'. Now if my biddies only do well by me this next week! I shall want quite a lot of eggs beside what I put into cake.

"I guess one—two—three's the most reliable rule for me, and it divides up well too. I shall want a plenty of hearts and rounds for the children. Poor things! What would Abby Richardson ha' said to see her own grandchildren made as little of as they have been this last three years? And their stepmother's as touchy as can be about things, too.

"I wish I could do something before Saturday; but I can't, only fix the baskets and get the other little presents ready. I hope Grandma Baker will like the pattern of that print I've got for her, and that Marm Norcross, up at the Farm, won't think black and white's too sober for a shoulder shawl. 'Twas all they had, but sometimes those poor-house folks is the most particular of all. Poor things! I suppose it's all they can do.

"I know Auntie Stetson will be real well pleased with that big-print Bible. It's the best one I could find that I could anyways seem to afford, and I hope she'll live to take lots of comfort with it. And I've got a little more shopping to do yet, if I can manage it.

"There, them pies are done, and it's eleven o'clock, though I guess this clock is a half-hour ahead. Lucy Hurlburt, you must step around if you mean to get red up afore dinner!"

She replaced the bowl carefully, put away the results of her baking, took her broom and dustpan, and went briskly up the winding stairs, looking in her scant gingham dress, wide apron, and frilled sweeping-cap, under which a pair of bright, dark eyes peered, like the traditional old woman who "swept the cobwebs out of the sky."

She worked with an energy you would hardly have given her credit for, singing meanwhile snatches of sweet old hymns, some of them long ago fallen into disuse, some as dear to this generation as to those in whose ears they were first sung. Her task was not a long one, and the last firm strokes of her broom made a not unseemly accompaniment to the low, fervent strains of

"Sun of my soul, thou Saviour dear."

It was evidently a favorite, and she sang all the verses through, though the sweeping was finished before the singing was. But it was not yet twelve, even by the kitchen clock forced against its will to "take time by the forelock," when she emptied the contents of her dustpan into the kitchen stove, and after a reassuring glance into the steaming stew-kettle which betokened dinner, sat down for a few minutes' rest before completing her preparations for the savory meal.

"Almost everybody keeps Christmas after a fashion," she soliloquized; "and sometimes in a good sort of fashion, too. But Easter, that makes sure all that Christmas brings, and brings so much comfort of its own besides, especially to folks that are old, or sick, or lonesome, missin' the ones that ain't with us; and there's a good many of that kind of us in the world. Easter somehow gets passed over with extra flowers and music in churches, and maybe a sermon that the folks that needs it most can't get there to hear. I can't think the Lord is real pleased to have it so.

"And then," she resumed, "for all that Easter calls to mind so much that's precious, and the real comfort and strength of it ain't to be told by most of us, I rather imagine that a good many folks that's troubled and sorrowful, even with actual griefs, have to work out their own peace and consolation, if they ever have any, same as they do their salvation.

"I should ache the worst way if I couldn't do something on Easter day that I think maybe my dear ones would ha' done or like to have me do for somebody they set store by when they was here."

A voice interrupted her soliloquy here, that of Asa bringing a last load of "light birch" from the wood-lot. She saw him bring his sled into position for unloading, and drop the thills as he freed old Jerry from the traces, an act which was always to her, accustomed to estimate almost to a minute the time required for each item of the "chores" indoors and out, a signal to place the dinner on the table; and she rose now, a strain of one of the hymns she had been singing coming involuntarily to her lips.

Six days later at the same hour she sat in the same chair, lingering to watch an interview in the yard at the side of the house. A sleigh with a single occupant, who had reined in his steaming horse at the Hurlburt homestead on some important errand, evidently, now seemed waiting for Asa's answer.

"He's coming into the house. I'm doubtful if it ain't bad news of some sort," she murmured, rising to meet her brother at the door.

"It's Jabez Pearson over from the Forks," he said. "Mother Purdy's been havin' congestion, and she's got a relapse just as they thought she was out of danger. The woman that was takin' care of her was called home by sickness, and they hain't got nobody to look to. Most everybody round there's been sick and kind o' pindlin' now, he says. So they thought they'd see if you wouldn't come over and spell 'em a day or two."

Miss Lucy's face fell and Asa went on :

"I don't s'pose you need go unless you feel to. An' I don't think you be very well able. He's on his way to the lower village to get Dr. Stearns. They thought 'twould be best for him to see her. And he says, if you don't feel like goin', he'll try to get Jane Martin to go over. Or he'll call for you when he goes back along."

By this time our friend's mind was made up. "Tell him I'll be ready," she said. "And, Asa, you'd better come in to your dinner now. I shall want to get well red up to leave things."

The next two hours were busy ones, yet not too full to leave room for real and grievous disappointment. The day following she had planned to take almost entire for the carrying out of her cherished plans, which she had hoped also to have set forward that very afternoon.

"And these two days are all there is. If I'd ha' known I could ha' had things ready, most all of 'em; and what I couldn't get Jabez to carry round I could send afterwards. It doesn't seem hardly right after all I've done. And I s'pose Jane would have gone, and done well enough; leastwise, they'd never know the difference. But I know Jane's apt to be careless, and she ain't used to sickness either, of that kind. I don't see but it seems to be for me to do. Maybe," with a little smile, "my Easter work ain't just what I thought it was, after all. And," while the smile gave place to a sweet seriousness, "it is ourselves that we are to give first and chief, 'by the will of the Lord.' It's something to have Him willing to show us how."

She had hardly heard of Good Friday, and had indeed not remembered that that day was the anniversary of the sacrifice in which she believed so devoutly. But I am sure the spirit of the day was in her heart as she went about her hasty preparations.

So "beforehand" was she with her house-keeping—this week even more so than usual—and in such spotless order was the house kept from day to day, that there was really time at last to tie and mark the parcels whose contents were ready to fill two baskets for two or three sick and aged women whom she could not bear to slight, and after some hesitation to cut some of her choicest flowers to carry with a box of honey and a jar of her best peach-preserves to Cousin Martha. "I guess they'll be needed there as much as anywhere," she reflected, "Martha never does have the best o' luck with her canned things, and she's no hand with plants, either. And it seems to be her I'm set to do for just now."

A belief which was much strengthened by the condition of things at the Purdy homestead when she arrived there late in the afternoon. Mrs. Martha Purdy was a far-away cousin of the Hurlburts, and not a favorite with either of them, though they seldom expressed the feeling, even to each other.

It was no surprise to Miss Hurlbut to find the house in a mild state of chaos, the children untidy, the pantry ill supplied—though James Purdy was in truth "a good provider," in the homely speech of the countryside—and the sick woman herself in her cheerless north bed-room with its far from dainty appointments, forlorn and unhopeful as well as seriously ill.

The verdict of Dr. Stearns, who followed close upon their own arrival, was, however, really encouraging. Perhaps the more so because he knew the "good care" he insisted on was sure to be given during Miss Hurlburt's stay, and that the better order of things she would surely bring about would be likely to last until his patient was convalescent, and when the momentum of the disease was spent it would not so much matter. And, indeed, he was not out of sight before Miss Lucy had begun the mild revolution that must precede her own benignant reign, making Mrs. Purdy comfortable with soothing remedies and well arranged pillows and reassuring words and per-fectly made gruel ; then while she slept steal-ing away into the kitchen to bake a tin of soda biscuit and another of gingerbread, and pre-pare a "raising of white bread" for the family table, leaving affairs there so that Effie, a girl of fifteen, and, as Miss Hurlburt mentally con-cluded, "real willin', if anyone could take hold with her or even show her about things a little," could carry them forward easily toward an inviting meal. "For I don't want 'em all sick," Miss Lucy said to herself.

She did not find much opportunity for soliloquy here, however, except such reflection as would suffice to shape her plans for immediate services. But there was time to wonder in the night watches if Asa "would carry those things right away after dinner, or towards night. I told him, in the afternoon, if I didn't come. And there's no prospect of my getting back to-morrow. And I guess it's just as well. I might be mean enough to go if there was a good chance, and Martha was doing well, and the nurse came back; and, however things go, there's one day's work for me here. I'm sure o' that."

The Saturday was a busy day, though she got little sleep the preceding night to prepare her for its endeavors. It was such a satisfaction, however, at nightfall to see the family rooms clean and tidy, the pantry well replenished, Mrs. Purdy comfortably settled in a clean spare bed in a snug south bedroom off the well warmed sitting-room instead of opening into the often noisy kitchen, and so far lifted out of her despondency that she could say gratefully, "I shall get well fast here, I know," while the newly developed energy of the daughters and the contentment of the husband were hardly less promising, that Miss Hurlburt well nigh forgot her own unusual exertions and even her aching head and limbs as she looked around her.

In the early evening the nurse returned, and Miss Lucy realized with a sigh of relief that her own "stent" was done, though it was not till late noon of the next day that she entered her own door. It was too late then for the Easter service she had been anticipating so long, too late to send her flowers for the pulpit, or even to brighten one or two sick rooms she had remembered. Indeed, she could only look around the familiar rooms, stroke her cat, caress her plants, look into the closet where her parcels had been—empty now, they had been delivered—and greet Asa just come from meeting, before she had to surrender to the blinding headache which had been gathering, and lie for some hours in her own room, dumb with the pain. And yet not unhappy, for the day's peace seemed to infold her even then. And at sunset the pain grew stiller and she came feebly out to her own chair.

"Better, are ye?" said Asa, coming in. "That's good! It's ben pretty lonesome here

lately for me and the cat. What time I was
here I went round with your things, and everybody was mighty pleased. What made you
think o' so much? Then I went over to see
Squire Perkins, I had some business with him.
Fact is, Lucy, I've changed my will. I thought
it over, and I concluded I could afford to give
up a little, so I left the Stebbins place to Josiah.
And then, seein' as it might never do him any
good so, I went around and talked things over
with him, and we made a little bargain, not a
bad one for him anyhow, and he's going to live
on't till we can be better suited, one or both
of us," and the old man smiled with a grim
satisfaction.

"O Asa," said his sister, "I can't believe it !"

"It's true, though," he answered. "I thought
maybe ye'd like it," he went on shyly. "Fact
I don't know's I should a' done it, leastways
just now, if you hadn't set me thinkin'. Though
'twould a' ben as well, like enough, if it had
come about quite a spell ago. But bygones
is bygones, we've both agreed," Asa said in
unusual confidence, then backed shyly out of
the room on a pretext of belated chores.

Miss Lucy sat quite still and almost raptur-
ously happy. The transaction of which her
brother had just told her implied not only the

adjustment of an old dispute begun long ago in a difference that had almost amounted to a quarrel between their half-brother Josiah and himself; it involved a generosity on Asa's part that gave far more than the other had, perhaps with justice, asked for vainly many years before, and, failing to obtain, had been as a stranger in the old home ever since. It had been the skeleton in Miss Lucy's closet all this time, and had often made her kindest deeds seem to herself but a pretense and mockery. Now how different all would be!

"And Josiah's wife's brother 'tis that's those children's father. She's their own aunt, with not a chick or child of her own, and she thinks a sight of 'em. Well now, they'll be at the farm a good share of their time, and not want for anything, I'm pretty sure. That's more than the cakes I fretted over, sure. We never know what the Lord of Easter is going to do with the gifts we try to bring him. To think of what we put in and what comes up out of it makes anyone think it's a little bit of the Resurrection come already!"

WHY NOT?

Penn Gorman's work basket was empty. It stood beside her in one of the sunny windows of their dainty sitting-room, with not so much as a torn handkerchief or frayed-out collar visible within it. And she, an earnest-looking, bright-eyed woman somewhere between youth and middle-age—just where, some of her dearest friends did not know or care—twirled the last pair of neatly darned stockings into a comely roll, and tossed it across the room to keep company with a little pile of clothing, freshly aired and waiting transferal to bureau and closet.

"Two o'clock of a Tuesday afternoon, and the very last stitch of mending done," she said impatiently. "And I've no earthly thing to make or mend, or alter. Is it any wonder I feel wickedly idle? Of course there are things we need if one had money to shop—shirts for

Prescott, and some winter sheets, and a table-cloth or two."

"But we are in no special need," said the other occupant of the room, a sweet-faced, fragile woman, in an invalid's chair. A crutch leaned against the chair's arm, and the hands were warped and twisted with rheumatism. They let fall, now, for a moment, the gray sock she was knitting. "And why can't you read, or paint, or rest? It's lawful leisure, Penn, and that never hurt anybody. People don't generally have enough of it."

"Some people, and sometimes. But it's like a good many other delightful things—to be appreciated only at intervals, with plenty of the other thing between. Really, with Prescott's busy time over, and the fall work so well done, with the long evenings and stormy days before us, I feel as though I were going to be lawlessly, inanely, drearily idle, unless I can find some hitherto neglected duty under my nose, so to speak. If there were a Woman's Exchange within a hundred miles, or any demand anywhere for such things, I'd go to doing fancy-work, though it isn't in my line, and I don't half like it. Or if I could get copying! 'Twould be so nice to make these unoccupied hours yield me a few dollars of even dimes!

You see mother dear, it would be so good to have just a little more money to use and give—especially the latter—there are so many ways!"

"You miss your salary," and the mother sighed. She felt sometimes her helplessness—this "prisoner of the Lord." These years of weakness and pain followed close on years that had been crowded with activities.

"Ah, yes," returned the other lightly, "and a good many other things that I had away from home and teaching. The cold mornings and going out in all weathers, and working at night; and being among strangers; and eating boarding-house fare, and the dyspepsia it created! You know I'd rather be here, with you. But, as I said, though we've all we need, I should like to have a little more money to spend and give. I'd like to do more in the church, for instance. There's so much needed, and I'm afraid Mr. Oaks's salary runs behind too often. And the collections aren't what they ought to be, for missions and other things, nor maybe the interest, either. I suppose the people do and give all they can, just as we do. Though, indeed, some of the ladies that could perhaps do a little more, are seldom out save Sundays, not always then. They are so busy with their housekeeping and their babies, and the children in school. They have enough to do, you see. But some of us have so much more time than money, I wish it were like Bible times, when the 'women that were wise hearted did spin with their hands' for the furnishings of the tabernacle. Our little church is getting so shabby inside ! And I don't wonder women are driven to having fairs and festivals and the like, to raise church-funds ; though I am glad they've given up such follies here. In my present state of mind, an affair of that kind would be a great temptation."

"Mother," she added, a moment later, peering out of the window, "I'm quite sure I see Auntie Graham coming down the hill, and I *think* she has her big work bag on her arm, which means, that she's got her patchwork and will sit an hour or two with you. So if you don't mind, after I give you your glass of milk I'll run over to Nina's for a little while. And I'll take my thimble. Her work-basket won't be empty, it never is ; and maybe I can lay hold on some of the wee stockings, or one of Johnnie's jackets or Madge's aprons, while I stay. You don't know how those children go through their clothes. One would think they walked with their elbows and danced on their knees."

Ten minutes later, Penn sat in Mrs. Nina Storer's dining-room, where that busy little matron was vibrating between sewing machine and cradle, with occasional *detours* to the kitchen. The mending basket, as Penn had predicted, was not empty. It stood even then on the table, crammed with torn trousers, out-at-elbow jackets, rent aprons, buttonless waists, and frayed-out skirts, for the week's wash had just come home and been sorted, and the clothing of eight, including five restless, romping children, was represented therein. The stocking bag lay near, also full to repletion, while the mistress of the house was, as she said, putting new binding on the children's winter skirts, which they must have at once.

"I'll clear away that rubbish in a moment, Penn," she said. "Mrs. McManus brought the wash early this week."

But Penn laid detaining hands on bag and basket.

"Not yet, please! Why, Nina, I'm suffering for work, and I like to mend. These stockings are enticing! And if you don't let me, I'll go off and spend the afternoon at the parsonage. Maybe Mrs. Oaks will let me mend *her* baby's stockings. I can do them beautifully," she added, whimsically.

"I know you can, and I hate to see you waste your time over such a bad lot as this. The children do wear out things so, and I've been so busy with house-cleaning and other work that had to be done, I've had to leave it, sometimes, or some of it. You see," she went on, "I just like to do my housework, and get on nicely with what Mrs. McManus does off and on. But when that's done, I do need my time to rest and be companion to the children and talk a bit with Loring when he comes home, or chat with a friend if one comes in."

"Indeed you do !"

"And, instead of that, I have to toil on over the mending and plain sewing, maybe till eleven o'clock or later. Evening is my best time, you know, with the little ones safe in bed. And I don't *look* at a paper, though Loring does read me bits. And as for going out to prayer-meeting, or a social, or the ladies' society, or the mission circle, or to make a call, why, it's out of the question !"

The conversation wandered then to other things, but a daring idea was growing in Penn's brain. It came forth at last.

"Nina," she said, "why don't you get a mender ?"

"A mender! I never heard of one. How much are they? I don't believe we could afford it?"

"You might hire one," said Penn soberly.

"Hire one?" echoed Mrs. Storer again, and Penn's laugh rang out merrily.

"O Nina, Nina, you don't take a bit! I mean, get somebody, get *me*, to do your mending every week. I'd be delighted to."

"Really, dear," she went on, as her friend sat staring at her in astonishment, "I mean it, and it would help us both. I've been wishing for something to do that would bring me a little money, and I feel so idle, our work is so light, and I do enjoy mending and plain sewing."

Mrs. Storer considered :

"Why, if you aren't in fun and would be willing, and if it isn't imposing on you, I'd be enraptured! The boys shall bring it to you regularly as soon as the clothes come home. I'm a month behind now, if you want to do the extra."

"Indeed I do."

"And then there's about so much every week."

And then they settled to the consideration of quantity and compensation, which details were most admirably arranged.

12

"It's a beginning, mother," Penn said, an hour later, as she recounted her plan in the quiet room flooded now with sunset light. "Not such a *very* small one either. For I plucked up courage after that to call at Mrs. Adams's and suggest a similar arrangement in her behalf. I knew she was equally busy, and she proved to be equally glad of the help. These two will be about all I can look out for. But Susie Stone was in there—I wasn't sorry, I believe I rather gloried in letting her know I didn't feel it to be beneath anyone to do—and I know *she* got an idea or two, also. She remarked that some of the ladies on their side of the village were complaining of being unusually busy this season. I shouldn't wonder if Sue found out that she could help them and not lower herself any either. She has more time than I. And example, even that of such a one as your humble daughter, goes a long way sometimes."

And so it proved. A bit of wholesome leaven had been introduced into the life of the little town. It worked in more than one mind, and stirred to activity, economic and benevolent, more than one pair of hitherto listless hands. Some over-tired mothers rejoiced in lightened tasks and lessened burdens and larger leisure, and church and society were gainers thereby. Unwonted faces filled empty spaces in the prayer meetings, and voices grown unfamiliar in long absence, were heard once more in woman's meeting and mission circle, while many a little, helpful gift, earned in these humble ways, came into the Lord's treasury, or went to aid His poor.

Penn smiled contentedly as she saw it all, and if she did not say aloud, "I began it," I am quite sure she thought it, and was thankful.

DEACON FAREWELL'S THANKSGIVING.

The east was all aglow with the approaching sunrise. Far around to the north and south the heralding color ran; and up into the azure sky, arching its dusky canopy over Smallridge, the waves of crimson went. The wind-clouds in the west, touched with the hastening brightness, rolled themselves together and disappeared. On the distant and leafless woods, on the scattered spires, and on the windows of the farthest houses, the radiance fell; while the nearer farms, and the village between the hills, lay in shadow. But in a moment more the sunlight reached them, also; and every pane twinkled, and every leaping brook smiled back to its smile. One by one the morning lights were put out, and here and there the smoke of some belated fire began to curl lazily upward, though most of the chimneys in the region had been breathing an hour and more.

Just as the first level rays of the sun reached the panes of a yellow house looking southward from the eastern slant of the ridge, a little woman within pulled up the curtain, and looked out with a face as bright as the sunshine itself.

"Sun's up, and I'll put away that lamp," she said briskly ; "and I do believe"—turning again to the window and then back to the table where her husband sat—"that we're goin' to have beautiful weather for Thanksgiving and maybe all the week. Now, Nathan, just let me give you some more coffee, and you hurry up with the chores, or leave 'em for Abner; and you get around early to invite the folks. And send up those spices you forgot, and some more raisins and citron from the store as you go along, will you, Deacon?"

The Deacon looked blank.

"I'll send up the spices, certain, 'Mandy. But I thought we was going to eat our Thanksgiving by ourselves this year,—not havin' any own folks near by, either of us. Though if you want to ask your third cousins over in Say-nood"—

"But I don't," interrupted his wife, impatiently. "Though I've no sort o' notion of sittin' down to eat the dinner you've raised, and I'm a cooking,—and everything in plenty, and all so nice,—just our two selves ! An' as for havin' folks, why, we haven't any nearer than Michigan,—and yet again *we hev*."

The Deacon looked more mystified than ever.

"There *was* my half-brother over to Katurik, but *he* died four years ago. There's his widow"—

But his wife interrupted him again :—

"Only night before last, in prayer-meetin', Deacon Farewell, you prayed for our afflicted brother, meanin' Jotham Swift that lost his daughter six months ago, and our brother sorely tried, which was Silas Wiggin whose barn burnt down with his hay, and so on ; an' for our bereaved sisters, the widow an' fatherless, meanin' Mis Carr an' Susie. An' every night you pray for all our brethren and sisters in the church an' in the Lord. An' you talk about the fathers an' mothers in Israel, and you say some of them converts . that you've pleaded with, and prayed for, and watched over, seem like your own children"—

"Spiritually, yes, they do, spiritually," interpolated the Deacon. "But they've got homes and family circles of their own."

"Not all of 'em. Why, Deacon, you know there's nigh a dozen you could think of, that it

would be a real Christian, brotherly kindness
to ask here."

"They'd be welcome, and they know it,
'Mandy; but Thanksgiving's different."

"*How* do they know it? Not by *your* tellin'
'em; an' I *know* Thanksgiving's different!
Why, Deacon Farewell, can't ye think how
much good 'twould do Mis Carr herself, and
Susie, especially, poor crippled thing, to have
a good, hearty, cheery visit, and eat Thanksgiving away from home, and get up, maybe, a
little heart and courage again? An' you pass
'em the bread and wine at the Lord's table
every month. And there's Moses Freeman."—

"But I'd have to ask Eben too."

"And what's to hinder, but your own pride
and contrariness? An' you two coming together
every communion Sunday, and between whiles
holdin' on to that old, worn-out grudge, or
pretendin' to. For I don't believe either of
you holds hardness now. And there's Ned
Kirke, come here to work in your mill, an' in
your Sunday-school class too. An' I'm going
to have two of my class, Lena Snell and
Maidie Burns, anyway. For they've only their
boarding place to stay in, holidays an' all
days, an' the woman ain't over pleasant or
particular. *I've* asked *them*."

"And quite right of you, I'm sure," rejoined the Deacon, pulling on his mittens. "Well," he went on, "if that's all, I don't see why we shouldn't have 'em, an' I'll try to see 'em this mornin'. I s'pose it's time."

"It's high time," answered his wife. "But that *ain't* all. If I was you, Nathan, I'd make up my mind to ask over Hiram Stirling and Mrs. Stirling. They're all alone, same as we are, only their sons are dead instead of off doing for themselves out West, as ours are. And the daughter, she's been in Californy these fifteen years, and has got to live there, if anywhere. You *must* ask *them*, Deacon!"

A pleading wistfulness had crept into her brisk voice, and she lifted her eyes beseechingly. But his eyes were turned away, and at that moment came Mrs. Mullens to help with days' works in the Thanksgiving preparations. And the Deacon, still and astonished, went about his chores, while the sharer of his joys and griefs and blunders and regrets looked after him anxiously.

For the daring little woman had set her husband a hard task, and she knew it; but she had long ago come to the conclusion that it must be done, and she knew very well that all that made it hard lay in the Deacon's own heart. The Stirlings, also, were fellow-members with themselves in the little church at Smallridge. They had been life-long neighbors and friends till there had been an unfortunate disagreement about church-matters, which had ended in a long and sullen estrangement. Mr. Stirling was hasty, but generous and easily placated. But Mr. Farewell was slow, self-reliant, and determined, even, his opponent said, to self-righteousness and obstinacy, though he was a believer and a Deacon, yes, and an honest, earnest disciple. And after the first heat of the discussion had cooled, the Deacon had let fall certain cutting words which he would have given much to recall, and which Mr. Stirling had felt then that he could never forgive. It had happened long ago, but the scar remained, and the wound still smarted.

So the little woman turned to her work with a prayer in her heart. And all day long amid the chopping of mince meat, the grinding of spices, the stoning of raisins, the stirring of pumpkin, and sifting of squash, the grating and pounding and beating, the flaking and baking and frosting,—that filled the old house with unwonted noises and savory smells,—she was thinking, "If it only could be."

The Deacon's face at dinner was inscrutable. He had been kept at home all the forenoon, first by a brother deacon, come to discuss ways and means and the church debt; then by a fellow selectman and member of the school-committee. The spices had been sent for and brought by the hired man at ten o'clock. So his wife could not tell yet what he meant to do, though she was quite certain that, at least, all save the last-named of the guests she was fain to welcome, would be asked and would come. Beyond that was uncertain.

And, in truth, the Deacon's intentions were hardly clearer to himself. He set out after dinner, driving slowly, and turning his horse, at length, in the direction of "Freeman's Lane," where the brothers Freeman lived together and, save for an old housekeeper, alone. Eben was in the yard as the Deacon drove up, and his round, ruddy, genial face invited an over-ture of friendship. Indeed, his hand was stretched out in greeting and in amity as soon as Deacon Farewell's own, and all lingering "hardness" was crushed once for all in that strong pressure. And when Moses joined them, a little later, it seemed but natural to proffer and second his wife's invitation, and as easy for them to accept it.

An hour later,—so fast time flies when one gets to talking !—our friend drove more swiftly out of the lane, shaded by leafless maples, and bordered with sere and withered grasses, and turned downward. Old Dobbin felt the brighter spirit behind him, betraying itself in the firmer grasp of rein, and cheerier "get up" of the familiar voice, and trotted on briskly. And, indeed, his master's heart was far lighter, and his sympathies far warmer already.

And then he stopped at Mrs. Carr's gate, giving, with much more than his usual heartiness, his wife's message to her. And he was both pleased and touched at the glad surprise that lighted their faces. Thence he drove around by the mill to see Ned Kirke; and when his errand there was done, the afternoon was spent. So, telling himself that he must be at home to see about the chores, for Abner might not have gotten home with the young cattle from the hill pasture, and putting by, as well as he could, the thought of another call he was to make, he turned homeward. Mrs. Farewell was watching for him, and Abner came to take the horse so he could go in immediately.

"Are they coming, Nathan?" she asked, as she took his overcoat, and brought his slippers.

"Yes, that is, Mose and Eben are. They wanted me to thank you kindly for the invitation. And the Widow Carr said she and Susie would be greatly pleased to. And Ned Kirke will be here, I expect." Here the Deacon stopped, and began to look around for his newspaper.

"And Hiram Stirling?"

"I—I didn't go up there; I hadn't time."

He had found his newspaper now and entrenched himself behind it. Mrs. Farewell was a wise woman, and she said no more, either then or next morning, when he drove away again, this time to Amesboro, on business, he said. He had been more than usually silent, and she knew not whether his mind was yet made up. "Maybe it's a-making," she said to herself, "an' I won't disturb it, for like enough it's the Lord's own dealing." A kindred thought was stirring in the Deacon's heart, and he hardly knew whether to be glad or sorry that he could no longer be content with the old offense between himself and his fellow-Christian. And his Bible had its word for him. This very Tuesday evening, as he read, a verse had almost stopped his utterance, "By this shall all men know that ye are my disciples, if ye have love one to another." As the Lord had questioned the repentant Peter, so he seemed saying to this other faltering follower, "Lovest thou Me?" And when his very soul cried out in the answer, "Yes, Lord, thou knowest that I love thee!" there came back the words of the other disciple whom Jesus loved; "He that loveth not his brother whom he hath seen, how can he love God whom he hath not seen?"

All through the wakeful night these words, and such as these, were repeating themselves to him, till the morning found him with a very humble and determined heart, yearning after reconciliation with God and man, and for that light of God's face which, to the earnest, deep-hearted man, was more than life and all life's joys.

Hiram Stirling was in his barn door when the Deacon drove up. He knew how much those few broken words of confession cost the speaker, and he answered them with words as genuinely humble. A few minutes later, Mrs. Stirling, rolling out pie-crust in her kitchen, was interrupted by the entrance of the two men, very plainly friends once more; and still more surprised to hear her husband say, "You needn't hurry about *your* pies, Susan, here's the Deacon to say that his wife wants us to take Thanksgiving dinner with them. We can, can't we?" On to Amesboro, now the

Deacon went, and did his errand, and drove home while the stars were shining, for the town was many miles away, and his business had taken time. But the way did not seem long, and the home-lights beamed out cheerily as he drove up the yard. And the little woman who stood all day long, in the midst of her sweeping and dusting, her cleaning and garnishing, had been praying and hoping and fearing, stood again in the doorway, and knew that all was right before she looked into his eyes or heard his glad "All's well !"

Ah ! home was very bright and its peace very sweet that night. The evening lesson had no rebuke, as they read their chapter, but only words of benediction. And on the morrow, when a glorious morning spread again its radiant light over Smallridge, there was a delightful stir of anticipation all through the homely house, reaching even to the stable and carriage shed. For some of their guests must be gone after, and, while they were about it, they might as well be carried to church in comfort, the Deacon said, bidding Abner get out horses and wagons, harnesses and lap robes, and sending him off in one team while himself and wife set out in the other.

No Thanksgiving service was ever quite so sweet to Deacon Farewell. In none had he ever joined so heartily, though his life had had its deliverances, like all of ours. Prayer and sermon and hymn were full of benediction,—a blessing with which was mingled no regret. And there came back to him, with a new meaning, certain words of Scripture, about "the sacrifices of thanksgiving."

His guests found him the most genial of hosts, and the saddest among them brightened in the good cheer of the homely feast. All differences were forgotten, with all incongruity; and as Mrs. Farewell watched her husband drive away at night with the last load of their visitors, she said to herself, "The Deacon seems as pleased as if he'd found a whole family of brothers and sisters,—an' I guess he has !"

GRANDMOTHER McLEAN'S VACATION.

Grandmother McLean was one of the silent ones; a small, quiet woman with gentle eyes and soft brown hair, in which each year the silver strands were a little more thickly threaded. So quiet was she that few dreamed of the strength and depth of her nature, her endurance, her tenderness, her self-sacrifice, her faith. The unceasing ministries and unfailing hopes of her long life told them all; yet many shared the willing services who did not stop to read or respond to the love that prompted them, or to consider if there were no needs or yearnings of hers they might help to satisfy. Seventy years ago and more, our Grandfather McLean had found her in a little village on the Massachusetts coast whither he had gone on some errand connected with his business of lumbering, and had straightway wooed and won her, a pretty, dainty, pink-cheeked maiden just seventeen. There was only her mother and herself, for her father was dead, and she the only child living, so when after two or three years of married life Amos McLean wanted to take his little family to his Maine home, a farm on a river flowing seaward among the inland hills, her mother, Grandmother Burritt, our great-grandmother, sold her little homestead and came with them.

It must have been "all for love," that hasty marriage which was such a happy one, for the husband was his young wife's senior by twenty years, and a stern man, and a silent one also. Almost as old as Grandmother Burritt, he outlived her only a few helpless years. Mrs. Burritt never revisited her old home, — in those days travel was slow and tedious. They had journeyed, when they came to Maine, in a covered wagon, emigrant-fashion, with their two gentle cows tied behind. If she ever longed for the old home-scenes, none knew. *She* was not one to complain either. They laid her to rest in the old burying-ground by the river, as she had known they must, though there was a vacant place for her beside a lonely grave far away in a little cemetery by the sea.

But I think, perhaps, she did not long so for the sight and sound and scent of the sea,

as did our own grandmother. *She* had heard
its murmur in her cradle, had played beside it
and with it, had listened to it in her musing
maidenhood. There, to the sound of its waves,
she had heard lover's pledges and taken
marriage-vows. Its lullabies had mingled
with her own as she had sung her first-born to
sleep, and they sounded still beside him in her
fancy, for she had left a little grave in that
seaside cemetery.

Once or twice, long ago, she had gone with
her husband on business to a seaport town,
and satisfied, in some slight measure, her longing for the sea. But that was long ago. There
were many children and many cares of many
kinds. They were all men and women, with
children of their own; some of them living on
farms. around, some coming home, or sending
their sons and daughters to grandmother's for
vacation, this summer of which I write.

The old farmhouse,—a low, wide yellow
house, nestled down among great white lilacs,
and leafy maples, and drooping elms, its
green-blinded windows looking out at you as
you drove up the yard, like half-opened eyes,
—was always full and over-running in vaca-
tion-time. Perhaps grandmother herself was
to blame for that, she made them all so heartily

welcome, and took such infinite and smiling pains to make them happy. Back and forth, from cellar to cheese-room, from clothes-press to chamber, from pantry to kitchen, you could hear the steady "trot" of her tired but willing feet. And she gave just as cordial greeting to Joel's widow, with her three children, who could make no return for her hospitality, as to the household of John, the successful man of the family. Lois, now a woman of forty-five, was the only one who remained unmarried. It had seemed probable, once, that she would be mistress of a fine farm in the neighborhood. Its owner and occupant, Ansel Fletcher, had confidently hoped it would be so, but something, no one ever quite knew what, had estranged them. She went out sometimes as nurse, commanding high wages, by her skill and experience, but this summer she did not mean to leave her mother with the care of farm and house.

Early in June John had brought his frail little daughter, Jean, wasted with a winter's illness, to try the tonic of the air of the hills. And as soon as school was out, Jean's elder sister, May, and her brother Will, and the mother, had come. And Joel's fatherless children and their mother were there. And

Mahala, Mrs. Olney, with a daughter of eighteen, and a son a little older to follow by and by.

And of course the families of Mary and Martha,—matrons who lived in the neighborhood, and had long borne the names of Grey and Brownlee, were often with their cousins "at grandmother's."

The young people were all together in her cool sitting-room one afternoon late in July. Harry Brownlee had come over bringing the mail; the most of it was for Uncle John, who sat down with it just outside the window, under the great oak tree in the yard, out of sight, but within hearing. There were also, letters for the young folks, and there was a lull in their merry talk while they opened them.

"Brother Charlie is coming Saturday," said Marian Olney, folding the letter she had read, and carrying it to her mother in the next room.

"And then we must have our excursion to the Point, and our picnic to the Oaks," said Harry.

"Right away, too," added his sister Nell, "for father and mother are going to take a little vacation week after next, and then we can't leave the house all day."

"Aunt Martha and Uncle Enoch going to take a vacation?" asked May McLean, with surprise in her voice. "Wonders will never cease. I thought they never had a day off."

"They're going to this year," rejoined Nell.

"Everybody takes a vacation but Grandmother," said little Jean.

"Where is Grandma, anyway," asked someone.

"In the cheese-room,—no, in the pantry making pies. Yes she is, Aunt Lois, you know had to go to Mrs. Horn's, who they say is dying, and Grandma has to do 'most everything alone."

"Grandmother wouldn't take a vacation, anyway," said Harry.

"Much you know about it," retorted Nell.

"Yes she would," said May thoughtfully. "Not a common vacation like ours, maybe, but there's somewhere she wants to go, or did,"—

"I know," said Jean, "back to where she used to live. She has told me so much about it! It must be beautiful there. It was lovely, long ago, and now ever so many folks spend their summers there."

"When I was a little girl, I remember," said Anna Grey,—she was fifteen now,—"one summer Grandma planned to go. She had sold a cow, and had money enough to do it, and Aunt Lois was to go with her, and Aunt Margaret was coming to keep house. But mother, and Aunt Martha, and Aunt Mahala, all thought Grandma was too old, and it was a great undertaking, and a long journey, off among strangers, and she gave it up."

"What a pity!"

"It was a shame!"

"So I always thought, but they said so much against it she didn't of course feel like going."

"She ought to go now."

"Perhaps she hasn't the money," said Minnie McLean.

"But we could raise it, among the children and grand-children, and she could go this summer, or September would be the pleasantest time."

The plan was noisily approved by the other young people, and Harry was appointed as collector, and Jean as treasurer of the fund, while May, Marian, Nell, Minnie, Will and Charlie were an advisory committee.

"How nice it would be for her to go and find out old friends and relatives. Maybe there'd be some nice cousins among them," said Nell.

"Grandmother was an only child."

"Second or third cousins, of course I mean, —and much the better," answered she saucily, with a glance that silenced quiet Will. "And then they'd be coming back to visit us."

It was resolved to begin at once, but Uncle John had heard it all, though they had forgotten his proximity, and with a remorseful remembrance of his mother's long desire, so many years forgotten and unsatisfied, had resolved, ere they were done talking, to himself take her back to that old town by the sea, under his own protection, and of course, at his expense, that very year. And he found opportunity to tell her about it that very night. He had seldom seen his mother so moved, as by the prospect of seeing again, so soon, her childhood haunts. Her tremulous smile, and brimming eyes, when she could believe he really meant it, touched him painfully. And he was the more resolved to make this holiday of a lifetime a happy one.

The cousins looked blank when Harry had found it out and came back to declare his occupation gone. But Nell said: "How delightful! Go ahead and get the money just the same, Harry, for she's got to have something to wear, you know. Do you suppose we'd let her go among strangers in that faded old black cashmere she'd worn this six years?"

"And the black silk that's as old as my mother," said Jean.

"And that big, old bonnet? Now we can get her something nice, and every one can help, if it's ever so little."

It was a pretty sight to see,—these maidens so anxiously intent on preparing grandmother's wardrobe, as interested as over their own dresses and hats. And it was pleasant, too, to watch grandmother, pleased, yet demurring, submit, with her serenity a trifle ruffled by the vexing vanities of basque or round waist, plain skirt or ruffled, watered silk or plain satin trimmings, to the innumerable discussions, councils, fittings and tryings on, that attended the making of the fabrics the children had bought, and the · mothers selected or approved.

Mrs. Joel, who was a dressmaker, had volunteered to cut and make, as her part, and her taste proved excellent.

"Grandmother's going to look ever so nice," said Marian one day, over the ruffling she had offered to hem.

"Of course she is," said Jean.

"But I never knew before," said Nell, "that she liked pretty things so well. She goes along and smooths and pats that black silk (and it *is* a beauty!) and watches Aunt Grace at her sewing, as pleased as a child. The cashmere's ever so nice for travelling, and the wrap Uncle Enoch and Aunt Martha sent for and gave her, is just as pretty and lady-like as it can be."

"Grandmother really cried over that," said May, "she was so pleased and surprised."

"But I think she was just as pleased,—a little childish, may be,—over the lovely laces and the collars, and the fine hem-stitched handkerchiefs you and your mother got."

"I don't know,—but have you seen the handbag the boys got her!"

"Yes, and that's fine, too."

From which bit of talk will be seen that the McLeans, having once made up their minds to do a thing, would spare no pains to do it well. And they made Grandmother ready with a thoughtful generosity that was a continued surprise, and a joy that was half a pain to her. She "wasn't used to having so much done for her," she said, and some of her children realized remorsefully how true it was.

It was the middle of September when they went. Aunt Lois was at home, and Grandmother could trust with her the house and the hens, the cows and the cheeses. Harry could stay nights. And had not Ansel Fletcher called one day to offer his services if in any

way they should be needed? He was brother
to Mrs. Harris, whom Aunt Lois had nursed
back to health, and it is possible Lois may
have met him there more than once of late.
Certainly there was that in the face or demeanor
of each that made Grandmother look at them
a little more keenly when she saw them
together that day for the first time in years,
and remember it while she journeyed. So
delightful a journey it was to Grandmother.
Jean and her mother accompanied them part of
the way, *en route* for the mountains. All the
other aunts and cousins had flitted homeward
ere that time. Every comfort and attention
that love could prompt or money furnish, Uncle
John lavished on her during that two days'
journey. He had insisted it should be broken
by a night's rest. And never bride or maiden
had a tenderer or more chivalrous escort. I
think, too, he was proud of his silvery-haired
mother, with her saintly face, her pure and
gentle speech, her ladylike dress and manners.
Strangers gave her admiring looks, and friends
all had courteous introductions in the crowded
cars or in the great hotels.

Arriving at the town which was their desti-
nation, he took her at once to the best hotel,
and installed her in a room which seemed to

her extravagantly luxurious. Every day he took her to see the places she had known so well, in an easy carriage, himself driving.

The town had become a populous little city, well-known also as a summer resort. But in that part where her home had been it was little changed. She found the old homestead sadly changed, it is true, but it was a satisfaction even to cross its threshold or sit in the yard. Indeed it was a joy to her, as she said, just to tread the old rocky soil.

They went to the little graveyard and she walked without hesitation to the old lot where her father and her child lay. Neglected it was, but, as Uncle John saw, a little care would restore it. He thought somewhat self-reproachfully of certain antiquarian researches and expenditures of his own, while those graves of his kindred had been unknown and neglected by him. And before they left town, the lot was in seemly and even beautiful order.

They had long drives around the rocky coast. The sea was the same; and the irregular cliff whose every turn and precipice was familiar to her. And it was an inexpressible delight to look out over the sea, and feel the saltness of the breeze.

They did not long remain strangers in the place. Making inquiries about families

Grandmother had known, some of them her cousins, he discovered that one gentleman whom he had well known, Mr. Allan, was quite a near relative, and he introduced them to others. There were only a very few old people whom Grandma remembered as young ones, but she found several delightful homes belonging to their children or grandchildren. They would not hear of her staying on at the hotel, after they found her out, and so Uncle John left her as their guest for a little while. The week she had planned to spend slipped away, and others with it, so it was nearly the middle of October when she came home. She was richer by memories and pleasures unnumbered, but she found herself somewhat poorer on her return. Mr. Fletcher, it seems, had renewed his suit, and, finding it successful, would wait no longer, and the quiet wedding was to be at once. It was odd that it should have happened in Grandmother's absence, so much of it, as if he and sober Aunt Lois had been young and bashful lovers. But the homeless aunt who was invited to take her place as Grandmother's stay, was only too glad to come immediately. No tongue could tell, and certainly not Grandmother's, unused to loquacity, all she had seen and heard and enjoyed during that trip; yet she did talk more than she had ever done before, there was so much to tell about it. And nothing delighted either her or the children more than for her to be entreated to tell them about her vacation visit.

There *were* cousins, and "nice ones," as Nell had hoped, who found their way soon to Maine, and came again and again. And some of the older friends came too. But Grandmother never went again, nor seemed to care to. The hived sweetness of her recollections of that month lasted all the remaining years. Nothing about it seemed to disappoint her. Perhaps the sweetness and serenity of her heart sweetened it all.

She began to fail slowly, yet perceptibly, not long afterward, and it was not many years longer that she was in the old home, for her gentle spirit had winged its way to the heavenly abiding places. And when her peaceful life ended, and she was laid in the graveyard where sounded only the low murmur of the river or the music of the pines, there was not one among her loved ones who mourned her so sincerely, who was not glad to remember Grandmother's one vacation, not one who did not wish the pleasure they gave her then had been many times repeated and multiplied.

The cousins, two or three degrees removed, who dwell on the Massachusetts coast, are not strangers now. Some of them, strange to say, are now more nearly connected with the McLeans. Other names have been given and taken. And only last year a young and lively lady went, not in an emigrant-wagon,—(we knew her as Nell Brownlee, but she is Nell Allen now),—to make good to Massachusetts the loss of that demurer maiden who came to Maine seventy years ago.

MISS HANNAH'S HARVESTING.

Miss Hannah Hoitt lived alone in a wide old house that had sheltered the families of her father and her grandfather before her. Its square, low-ceiled rooms were peopled, for her, with precious memories and tender associations. She would not shut the sunlight quite out of any of them, so that they all retained some pleasant look as of occupancy. And the rooms she really lived in were bright, restful, sunshiny, with enough of the old-time quaintness to give them a peculiar charm, and sufficient subserviency to newer fashions and fancies of adornment to assure you that the owner lived in to-day, rather than yesterday.

Miss Hoitt was much esteemed in the little community of Millton as a woman of means, of sense, of character, of generous purposes and practices. The farm had dwindled from its once broad area of tillage and meadow and pasture and woodland, to less than sixty acres. Yet it was large enough for her to manage, for she carried it on herself, with as careful and capable an oversight as was exercised by any of her neighbors on their domains. It was the standing wonder of the neighborhood and of the little town, "how Miss Hannah could 'manage' so well." Every spring the boldness and magnitude of her ventures astonished them. Every fall the quantity and quality of the crops she produced therefrom amazed them still more. Her beans and corn, her cabbages and cucumbers and onions, her beets and her asparagus, nodded to one another from their weedless rows in triumphant luxuriance. Her berries blushed in exultation. Her little orchard dropped its rosy and golden fruit gleefully. In truth, it was the garnering of her harvests that perplexed her. She revelled in the long days when she could dig and tend and water, and "see the things grow." But when the days grew short, and the first frosts came, and the pumpkin-vines grew black, and the potato-tops died, and she began to fear for her tenderer fruit, then despair and dismay began to fill her soul. For then her house-keeping tasks were more onerous, her neighbors could seldom be hired to help, and "help," proper, was "scarce." And, though Miss Hoitt was no scold, and didn't know how to whine, her voice was apt to grow plaintive as she sometimes related her anxieties.

Hers was a bright and busy life, in all its loneliness; and many a weaker or less hopeful heart shared its sunshine. She had not always expected to live thus alone. Once she had looked forward to a far different life. Perhaps it had been all the harder that her own hand had put aside her joys. But she couldn't have done otherwise, she would remind herself. There was only she to take care of the ageing father, the querulous grandmother, the invalid sister,—all gone from her long ago. And he, Allen Maynard, had his own brave life to live. She would not let him waste any of it waiting. She had sent him away, and perhaps she had not told him very clearly the reason why. But she had never ceased to think of him and pray for him. When she read that pathetic story of Miss Jewett's, "A Lost Lover," it came to her suddenly that *her* lover might have been "lost," to her, and the world, to goodness and God, as that man was. But she always said to herself that that could never have been. Wherever Allen Maynard was, she was very sure that he was still good and useful and brave and genuine.

Over her low threshold, above which hop-vines grew, and morning glories hung, from dawn till noon, their dewy chalices of purple and crimson and white, came one late September afternoon, her nearest neighbor, and one of her dearest friends, Mrs. Sterne. She was younger by a few years than Miss Hoitt, but loved, trusted, petted, even sometimes confided in, by the older woman.

"Come in, Lucy? What's the matter, child? Something worries you; and you're tired out, too. Now just go into the sitting-room and take the easy chair, and I'll be in in a minute, just as soon as I slip on my other dress.

"You see," she resumed, a little later, coming back freshly attired, "I've been trying to get in my grapes and pears, and some of my apples. I had to begin in season, and keep at it, a little to a time, and I'm wofully behindhand now; and help I can't seem to get, for everybody else is busy too. Now, Lucy, what troubles you, and what can I do?"

George Eliot remarks on the widely different meanings that may be given to those last four words by the tone and inflection with which they are uttered; expressing now heartiest sympathy and helpfulness, now the coldest of indifferent courtesy. But the words as Miss

Hannah said them, were full of the wish to help, and to know how to help.

"I don't like to tell you, Hannah; you have cares enough, without our rolling any of ours on to you. But Jotham's sister Emily, she that married a Swift, is sick with typhoid fever, the real, raging typhoid. They live over to Easton, you know, and there's nobody, hardly, to go, but me; and it seems as if I *must* go right off and stay till she's better. And there's only Mary Nelson, and she so young and heedless, for all I've had her a year and done my best with her, to learn her, to keep house. She could do well enough for Jotham and John, but Jotham's got men a coming right away,—the threshers, and carpenters to do his barn. That can't be put off. And the new superintendent in the mills, he promised certainly he'd board, because he used to know him, and it would be handy and homelike."

"And you want me to take 'em?" queried Miss Hannah.

"O Miss Hannah! we do hate to ask or let you. But what can we do? And Jotham says he'll get all your apples and potatoes and things in, in good season, and be glad to, and you shall have good pay for the men, if you

only think you could do it. And you don't
know what a relief it would be. You see,
we've got to take Emily's children home, till
she's better."

"Well, I'll try it, and, if nothing happens,
I guess I can carry it through."

"How is it, Hannah," went on the other,
"that most lone folks have enough to do to
take care of themselves? They think people
ought to do for *them*, and look out for 'em, and
especially when they get to middle age. But
it's always just the other way with you."

"I don't know," returned Miss Hannah, hesitating. "Yes, I *do* try to help other folks what
I can. And I don't see that I've ever been
any worse off for it. Truly, I think it's just
that keeps me up and gives me courage to
work. It's something to think of and plan for,
you know. Now, if I could only do for myself, I shouldn't feel as though 'twas hardly
worth while always, though that's something.
But when I can do something for someone else,
why, it makes me as strong again, and a sight
hopefuller."

"I don't doubt it. But now, Hannah, do
take care of yourself, and get somebody to
come in and help you. We can't let you get
worn out yet."

She did not look worn out as she flitted about after her visitor had gone, getting her cozy tea and putting things in order for the night. Energy was in every movement of her trim, spare figure, and a kind of hopeful content and courage blended with the kindliness and humor that illumined the brown eyes. She was adjusting herself mentally to the new turn affairs had taken; with that ready willingness characteristic of her. "I couldn't do differently," she was saying to herself. "There wasn't but me to do it anyhow; and the money will be a real help this fall. The house needs something laid out on it, and I want to send Martha's girls something by and by; and now I shall have a little more for missions, home and foreign, too; and I can get some of those books I've been wanting." And she paused in her flitting to and fro, to look lovingly at the already well-stocked shelves of the massive secretary, and thoughtfully at the empty space in the newer bookcase beside it. "Yes, I am not so sorry as I might be. 'Twill be quite a piece of work, though, before it's through. However, I guess I can manage."

"Quite a piece of work" it proved indeed, to be. The threshers came, staid a week, and departed. Close upon them came the carpenter's crew ; and just as they were well settled, came the most dreaded of all, Mr. Sterne's friend, the superintendent at the new mills. Miss Hannah had word that he was coming, and Mr. Sterne drove over with him at supper-time. He was in haste, and stopped only to say that his sister was no better ; the fever was having a long run. Lucy was about worn out, too. "And this is the gentleman we spoke of, Hannah, that you said might stop here a spell. I think he's an old acquaintance of yours."

And Mr. Sterne had driven off before she had had one good look at the man before her. He lifted his hat then and held out his hand with a smile.

"You used to know me, Miss Hoitt. You can't have forgotten how many times we've trudged up the hill to school together, and how many times you did my sums and helped me out with my parsing, in the little red school-house over yonder. Or, if you've forgotten, I haven't."

"Allen Maynard? I had no idea it was you that was coming ! I didn't really know *who* it was, come to think, but I didn't dream it was you !"

"But you'll take me just the same ?"

For answer she led the way into the house, with pink cheeks, shaking off her confusion as best she could.

The little home was very cheery. The slant rays of the setting sun streamed in between the plants in the bay-window and gilded the bindings of her books and made great reflections from the polished andirons. And in the next room was spread the dainty tea-table, with its crimson cloth, its glittering glass, its tempting array, and its vase of flowers in the center. For Miss Hannah was persuaded that even "those men" noticed and appreciated her flowers. And the fragrance of freshly-made tea, and inviting odors of browning biscuit, of baked apples, and other appetizing dishes, were in the air. And it was with pleasure not all concealed that the new boarder took the seat she assigned him. It chanced to be opposite her own. It was natural that the days should seem to go by faster than ever, now. They were very short, anyway, and Miss Hannah was very busy. If any other element gave a new, satisfying zest to day time task and evening talk, she did not own it.

Allen Maynard *was* still, "good and brave and generous," though his hair was turning gray, and he had been many times across the continent, twice across the sea, once, even around the world. He had many things to tell of people and countries and customs known to her only through books. And he liked books as much as she did, too, and brought some of his own for her to read, and sometimes new ones that they read together.

The work on the new barn dragged wearily, though Miss Hannah hardly noticed that October was gone and November was going, till one night she heard the men say that they should just about get done when the ground closed up; in time maybe, to get home before Thanksgiving. And Mrs. Sterne came home; her sister was convalescent, but she was well nigh worn out herself, with watching.

And now the carpenters would go in a week or two, at most, and Miss Hannah began to realize that the old life would soon begin again for her, and that it would be lonely. For Mr. Maynard must go, too. How should she let him know it? Her hints fell unheeded, and though the men spoke of going home, and she, of being alone once more, she did not see that he noticed.

But it was her turn to be surprised a little later, when he spoke of *his* plans for the winter, and of business in Easton.

He would not be near, then, even to drop
in of an evening! She began to be a little
lonely already. He had had a better position
offered him, maybe. And then she heard the
men say that Mr. Maynard was owner in the
mills, both at Millton and Easton. He had
acted as overseer here because he was needed.
Some one less capable would do now, for
affairs were running smoothly again, and the
Easton mills needed his attention. And they
said he had much other property there, besides.

One mild, sunny day,—an Indian summer
afternoon—he came with a carriage to take Miss
Hannah over to Easton for a ride. They drove
to the mills and around them ; then about town.
He drove slowly past a large, stately house,
suggestive of gracious uses and generous hos-
pitalities.

"I bought the place two or three years ago,"
he said. "I have never rented it. It would
make a pleasant home, would it not? Might
it not be our home, Hannah? I have kept it
for you. I have waited for you. Shall we
not have our Indian summer at last?"

So the question was asked and answered,
and a new life began, with brighter and warmer
and richer joys, and larger opportunities.

The neighbors had "always known that Miss
Hannah was smart; she had done better than

ever this year, too; but they hadn't expected, with all the rest, at her time of life, too, she would be harvestin' a husband."

THE SERMON DAVID TRAIN HEARD ON MEMORIAL DAY.

He didn't hear it at the Town Hall, for he didn't go there. None, save himself, heard it at all, and he was not listening for it.

David Train was not accustomed to keep Memorial Day in any way. And while his neighbors got out their carriages and washed their mud-bespattered wagons, and brushed and renovated their old clothes, or got themselves new ones, to go to "Decoration," *he* always planned to stay at home. He would have a bit of carpenter work about his barn or sheds, that must be done; or a piece of fence to put up; or a little late planting that he could leave no longer; and the faint roll of distant drums, the sounds of martial music coming through the pleasant air, and the rattle of hurrying teams as the country folks drove by, did not at all disturb him.

So you may infer, and rightly, that David Train was not a "public-spirited" man; nor had he quite the impulses or principles of an ardently patriotic person. He asked no favor, of place or patronage, of his country. Such little offices as had been entrusted to him in the town or county, he had not sought; and the duties thereof he had discharged with an honest fidelity that was above suspicion of greed or selfishness. Indeed, he was not a stingy, hardly a selfish, man. Or perhaps I should say his selfishness was rather a negative than a positive quality. He simply "minded his own affairs," and kept on in his own little round of his own duties and interests. Only, every year, as he grew older, that round of recognized duties grew narrower, and year by year the claims upon him, outside his own small household, had less hold upon him. When a neighbor would tell him of something in village affairs that ought to be righted; of town improvements that might be made; of a need, or a want, or an abuse, that earnest and honest men might do away with,—the suggestion was dismissed with the satisfied remark that he—David Train—"had no call to meddle." He had "no call"—or he heard none—to help improve and re-grade the schools, to secure a town library, to raise funds for a soldiers' monument. And, of course, he had no call, either, to join in the Memorial Day observances. His wife had always a great basketful of flowers and vines to send by some neighbor, for the ladies in the village to arrange. She saved jealously her geranium blossoms, her petunias, the blooms of her oleander, the early sown nasturtiums in her window boxes, and her roses. And she had the bloom of the early things that lived over in her little front yard,—snowballs and flowering almond, white lilacs, polyanthus, tulips and jonquils, and the lilies of the valley. She always sighed because Decoration Day came so early. A month or two later, her carefully tended flower-beds—a half-dozen they were, sown with all the simple, easily started seeds that thrive in dear, old-fashioned gardens—would be masses of bloom. Yet her contribution to the Memorial garlands was by no means to be despised. Her flowers were her one indulgence, and her husband always humored her in it, helping her in his clumsy fashion, and paying little heed, apparently, to the disposal or distribution of the flowers.

She, perhaps, would have liked to go to the Decoration Day services. Once in a while she did go, with one of her married daughters, or an obliging nephew. To-day she had no such opportunity, and after her housework was done, busied herself in her garden, around her shrubs and her herb-bed.

"I wonder," mused she, presently, "where David is? I thought he was a hammerin' out to the barn or somewheres, but I don't hear him. Mebbe he's gone over to the pasture, to build a fence or something."

He had gone across the fields, with hammer in hand and nails in his pocket, but it was not in the direction of the pasture. A few minutes later he might have been seen entering the little grave-yard, down among the meadows, beyond the railroad track. This little cemetery, he knew, had been visited by a delegation from the G. A. R. Post in the forenoon, and would doubtless be left to its usual solitary quiet the remainder of the day. It was not very much used, only by a certain section. It was quite large, however, and well kept, for a country grave-yard.

The week before, Mr. Train, who was a carpenter, as well as a farmer, had had a letter from Squire Rollins, whose boyhood home was near his own. Squire Rollins's business, and his home during the winter, were in another state and city. But he still came, with his family, to the old homestead to pass the summers. He was later than usual this year, but was coming soon; and friends who wanted to explore the region quite thoroughly, one of whom was, he said, "a bit of an antiquarian," were coming with him. He had wanted some things done about the home place, and had also asked his neighbor to go over to the grave-yard and mend the fence a little, and especially put in seemly order the Rollins family lot. The fence was not badly broken. A half-hour's work made it neat and strong. Nor was there very much to do on the Squire's lot. There were a few boughs, that had protected the ivies and the rose-bushes, to take away, and leaves and dead grass to be removed; fortunately he had brought a small rake with the hammer.

The place where his departed friends, neighbors, and kindred slept, had no terrors nor awful, depressing associations for David Train. He was a Christian, with a Christian's faith. It may be his belief was rather deep and high than broad and generous, yet it was a vital, sustaining, really consoling one. He did not follow it out to its full, grand, sacrificial, beneficent, reasonable development in all relations of this life. He did not realize and ful-

fill—who of us does?—the length and breadth
and depth and hight of love and service, which
should answer to "the breadth and length and
hight and depth" of "the love of Christ, which
passeth knowledge." But his faith was very
real.

The sunshine, the birds, the summer winds,
and "the green things growing," were all doing
their best to brighten the lonely quiet of the
spot. The grass was green upon the graves,
the sunshine flecked the sward. The winds
were breathing softly over the bending willows, and the willows themselves were very
tenderly green. Here and there a wild
flower peeped out, and a ground-sparrow
had hidden her home in a corner. The robins
had their nests in the elms all builded, and
some of them had leisure to sing right tune-
fully. "To-give-is-to-live—to-give-is-to-live!"
sang the merry-hearted bobolinks. "To-give-
is-to-live—to-give-is-to-live! For-giving-is-
living-you-know-ow!"

And everything around *was* giving something to the rest and to the world. Even the
solemn old pines, half-a-mile away, sent down
their healing fragrance by willing messengers,
—the winds.

David Train went to and fro about his work.
He had raked up the litter of leaves, and was

carrying it away. Here and there, in many lots, were fresh wreaths and bouquets, and the most of them were on those long mounds which were marked, with tiny flags, as soldiers' graves. He stopped sometimes, as he passed, to read the inscriptions on the head-stones. "He heard his Country's call," or "He gave his life for his Country," was frequently carved on the marble above such resting-places.

The names were nearly all of them familiar to Mr. Train. Some of them were of men who had died within a few years,—veterans of the war. Some of them had been there twenty years or more. David Train had not been a soldier. He did not volunteer, and he had not been drafted. Yet he had given,—rather should I say there had been wrenched from him in that time of strife and peril,—something more precious than his own service, or even his life. A younger brother, inexpressibly dear to the quiet, self-contained man,—for such he was even in youth,—had enlisted, in all the ardor of patriotic self-devotion. He had not lived to serve his country long. And *that* grim, flower-covered mound, with the gleaming marble at its head, held all that had come back from the Southern battle-field where he was wounded.

14

This had been the one deep, uncured sorrow of David Train's life. To only one other had the loss caused such anguish. Mary Neal, his brother's betrothed, saw the dearest hopes of her life go out, when the sad news came. But sorrow had, ere long, unlocked, enriched, fertilized her life. She was abundant in good works, many of them hidden, all of them unobtrusive, yet none the less real and beneficent.

After his work was done, David Train went to the corner of the burying-ground where slept his father and mother, long dead, and the sister who had died in infancy, beside that blossom-laden grave, whose stone bore the name of "Edward Train." It was yet early; he was tired, and the place was very still, so he sat down to rest. He fell to musing, as he not infrequently did, over what Edward would have been and done if he had lived. Sometimes he fancied him a minister in the pulpit; sometimes he saw him going to India, the Gospel in his hands; sometimes he appeared a heroic Christian pioneer in the far West. Oftener the elder brother imagined the younger one engaged in some form of missionary work at home; perhaps in a great city, perhaps in a scattered, struggling rural parish. "He'd have given himself away *somehow*, if he hadn't gone to war," sighed the musing man.

"To-give-is-is-*is*-to-live," sang that wise bobolink again; but his one hearer did not understand, so he flew away, and the man went on wondering. Wondering if, had circumstances so seemed to determine it that his brother had been, say, in his own environments,—been a busy, hard-working, prosperous farmer, as he was,—Edward would still have differed so from most of the world. What would he have to give then? Or, would he have been still giving? Yes, probably he would. There was Mary Neal, with much less; but she had something to give always. And when her purse grew lighter, too light to spare a copper, why, she gave her strength, her sympathy, her prayers, her time, what she had,—in short, *herself*,—the more abundantly. David Train was not rich. *Why* should *he* give? But he could not help thinking, himself, what a hard, cold place to live in the world would probably be, if no man cared more or did more, for his fellowmen, than he was doing. Where would be Nation and State but for these, and thousands. of others, who had given their lives for other men's liberties? Where or whence came eternal life for us, but through One who gave himself for us? "Hereby know we love, because he laid down His life for us, and we ought to lay down our lives for the brethren." The remembered words came of themselves: "Beloved, if God so loved us, we also ought to love one another."

The bobolink came back again, and was singing his happy carol over and over in the elm. But that wasn't the refrain that was running in David Train's mind. It was a line or two of some homely, familiar verses his wife had read aloud one evening. There was something like this in them :—

> "If your life ain't worth nothing to other folks,
> Why, what's the use of living?"

.   .   .   .

It was almost six o'clock when he left the quiet grave-yard. The country teams were coming back along the winding road,—hurrying home, for it was late, and supper was to get, and the chores to do,—when he went homeward across the fields. His neighbors had been thrilled by eloquent words, and had felt loyal and generous impulses stirred and strengthened within them. Grand orations had been pronounced in many places all around him, but David Train had heard none of them. Yet his Memorial Day lesson had found him, just the same. And from that day he began to find "the blessedness there is in loving and giving and helping."